Circle C Christmas Collection

Six Short Stories

Susan K. Marlow

Ⓒ CREAT!ONS

© 2022 *Susan K. Marlow*

Published by Circle C Creations
3 Box Canyon Road, Tonasket, WA 98855

All rights reserved. No part of this book may be reproduced, stored in a retrieval system, or transmitted in any form or by any means—electronic, mechanical, photocopy, recording, or otherwise—without written permission of the publisher.

The persons and events portrayed in this work are the creations of the author, and any resemblance to persons living or dead is purely coincidental.

ISBN: 978-0-9975067-8-5

Printed in the United States of America.

Contents

1. Andi's Christmas Good-bye *1876* 5
2. Andi's Christmas Blizzard *1877* 19
3. Andi's Interrupted Christmas *1878* 43
4. Andi's Christmas Ball *1879* 63
5. Andi's Icy Christmas *1880* 93
6. Andi's New Year's Gala *1882-1883* 147

1. Andi's Christmas Good-bye

Chapter One

December 1876
This story is set six months before *Andi Saddles Up*

Eight-year-old Andi Carter and her best friend, Riley, sat on the top railing of the corral late one Saturday afternoon in early December.

"You *know* I can rope better than you," Andi boasted. She clutched her worn lasso and grinned at Riley. "Leastways, I don't ever rope calves' hooves and get dragged around the cow pasture."

"That was two whole years ago," Riley said with a huff. "And at least I roped the calf. Why, you could barely rope at all back then." He grinned "You couldn't even rope Duke, but I—"

"I don't want to talk about roping ranch dogs." Andi frowned and clutched her lasso tighter.

"You started it." Riley gave her a playful shove.

Andi nearly flew from the top railing. Just in time she threw her arms around one of the tall posts. She hugged it and scowled at Riley.

They'd practiced their roping skills all afternoon. Andi's aim was nearly always straight and true. Her rope dropped over her pony's neck "slicker than grease," as Riley's Uncle Sid often told her.

Andi had roped Coco eight times this afternoon. She never missed, so long as he wasn't trotting too fast.

Riley was good at roping too.

But he's not as good as me. Andi sighed happily.

"All right, all right. I'll say it." Riley took a deep breath. "You rope better than I do, but—"

"You *always* have to add 'but' to everything I say."

"But . . ." Riley laughed. "I can trick ride."

Andi's happy thoughts dissolved quicker than a morning mist. Her friend told the truth about *that*. Why did Riley have to bring up such a sore topic on an otherwise perfectly good Saturday afternoon?

No matter how many times Andi begged Mother and big brother Chad to let her trick ride on Coco, the answer was always, "Trick riding is too dangerous for little girls."

Hmm, but not too dangerous for little boys? *No fair!*

Mother didn't seem to mind if their ranch foreman, Sid, had taught Riley how to trick ride. Ranch boss Chad didn't seem to care either.

But they both agreed that *Andi* would not trick ride.

She shivered a little in the sun's warm rays. Mother and Chad were probably remembering what happened to Father over two years ago. He'd been thrown from his horse and killed. Weren't they worried that Riley might fall off Midnight and be killed?

Apparently not. Chad never ordered his foreman to stop teaching his young nephew "dangerous" stunts.

"Hey, look!" Riley broke into Andi's thoughts. He gave a long, low whistle. "That's a mighty fine horse coming up your driveway. I wonder whose it is."

Andi twisted around on the railing and shaded her eyes.

Sure enough, a tall rider was trotting up the dusty Circle C driveway. Each step puffed the dust up and around his beautiful tobiano paint horse. The winter storms had not yet arrived to dump rain and turn that pesky dust to mud.

"Hey there!" the rider hollered. "Howdy!"

Chad, who had just strolled out from the barn, hiked himself up on the corral railing and returned the howdy.

The rider nudged his mount into an easy lope the last fifty yards of the driveway. He brought the paint horse to a stop alongside the corral.

Riley's hazel eyes widened. "Pa!" With a flying leap, the boy hurled himself from the top railing, and straight into his father's welcoming arms.

Andi watched, openmouthed. Two years ago, Riley's mother had felt well enough to spend Christmas with Riley, her brother Sid, and Andi's entire family. She had stayed on the ranch for two months, but Mrs. Carrie Prescott had eventually returned to San Francisco.

Riley had wanted to go with her, but she was still not completely healed from her consumption illness.

"Not yet, Son," his mother had told him sadly. "It won't be long, though. You like it here on the Circle C, don't you?"

"Oh, yes!" Riley answered. "Uncle Sid is good to me, and Andi's my best friend."

Mrs. Prescott had smiled. "Your father is so busy with the army these days that he's barely at the fort. Be patient."

"Yes, Mama," Riley promised. He'd waved a cheerful good-bye when she left, clearly happy for her long visit, but just as cheerful to be staying behind on the Circle C.

But now? Andi stared at the tall army captain in his blue uniform. Riley's father was here. What could this mean?

Maybe Captain Prescott had come for a visit, like Riley's mother had. Perhaps he was here to check up on Riley before going off on more army duties.

Why, oh why had Riley's father shown up today?

Andi didn't have to wait long to hear the answer to her worrisome, unspoken question.

"Why have you come, Pa?" Riley asked, hugging his father tighter.

Captain Prescott chuckled. "Don't you know, Son? I've come to take you home."

Chapter Two

Andi gasped and gripped the corral post. *Home?* To that big fort what's-its-name in San Francisco?

"You're taking me back to the Presidio?" Riley's eyes shone.

"For a little while," Captain Prescott said. "But I'm being transferred to Fort Alcatraz after the holidays. Your mother is feeling much better. We can be a family again."

Andi slumped. Riley couldn't leave the ranch. He just *couldn't*. Her friend had lived with his Uncle Sid on the Circle C for so long that Andi hardly remembered what her life was like before Riley showed up.

Had it already been three years? Every adventure in Andi's short life included Riley. Together they had gotten lost and then found by the Yokut Indians.

They had gone to the state fair two years in a row. Riley won third place when he brought mean Henry the rooster to the fair. He'd sat behind Andi on the long train ride and explained all about coal, and how it made the train go.

The only place Andi had gone and where Riley did not follow was school. Now, she wished Uncle Sid had made him attend so she could have seen him more often.

Hot tears stung her eyes. *Who will I play with all day?* No. Riley could not leave.

"It's nice to meet you, Miss Andi."

The captain's words jerked Andi from her spinning thoughts. Her head snapped up.

"What do you say?" Chad prompted. Clearly, he had introduced himself and his younger sister.

"N-nice to meet you," Andi stammered.

Inside she cringed. It was not nice to meet Riley's father *at all*. He was taking Riley away from her.

"Stay for supper, sir," Chad invited. "You, Sid, and Riley are welcome around our table for a going-away party." He ruffled Riley's brown tangles. "This is a happy day, boy."

"It sure is, Mr. Carter!" Riley crowed. Then he caught Andi's gaze. His lips pressed together into a straight line. Whatever he planned to say next stayed inside.

Andi dropped from the corral railing and ran for the barn. If she stayed one minute longer, Chad, Riley, and Captain Prescott would see her cry. She could not let that happen.

Slipping past the double doors, she climbed up the ladder into the hayloft and found one of Bella's kittens. Pulling the tabby-striped ball of fluff into her arms, she sobbed until no more tears poured out.

The afternoon dragged on.

Later, the December sun went down, bringing with it the chill of a clear, crisp evening. Still, Andi did not come down from the loft.

Thump, thump, thump.

The sound of footsteps echoed inside the quiet, darkened barn. Then came a swishing noise—the sound of hay tossed to half a dozen hungry horses. Whinnies, snorts, and snuffling were sounds Andi usually loved. Tonight, she ignored them.

A glow from the lantern shone below. It came closer, then up the ladder until Andi had to squint against the brightness.

A dark face showed from behind the yellow light. Andi couldn't tell who it was at first, but her oldest and favorite brother's voice gave him away. "Hey, honey. It's suppertime. Come down. We have guests."

"I know." She made no move to slide over to the edge of the loft. She scooped up an orange kitten and held him against her chest.

Instead of scolding her and demanding she come down *this instant,* Justin sighed. He climbed all the way up the ladder, brushed the hay away, and set the lantern down in a safe spot. Then he hauled himself into the loft.

He whistled. "I haven't been up here for ages." He spied a rope hanging from high above, secured to the barn's peak. "Same old rope we all played on. You and Riley have had hours of fun up here, haven't you?"

Tears threatened to spill, but Andi wiped her eyes before they could dribble down her cheeks. She nodded. "Riley found a giant spider's web up here the time Aunt Rebecca came for Christmas. You wouldn't believe how many spider were caught in that web!"

Justin smiled. "You caught them for your lizard Pickles."

"Most of them, anyway." Andi gave him a grin, but just a small one.

Justin settled against a wooden crate and looked at his sister. Then he took a deep breath. "You know, Andi, that this day had to come sometime. Riley's stay with his Uncle Sid was only supposed to last six months."

Andi's eyes widened. "Really?"

Her brother nodded. "When Mrs. Prescott couldn't shake her sickness, the doctors encouraged her to let her young son stay on the ranch until she was completely healed."

He scooted closer to Andi and put an arm around her. "Think how much Riley's mother missed him as the months—and then the years—went by. Think how much Riley must have missed his mother. Instead of drowning in your own sorrow, you should be happy that Riley can go home and be with his father and mother."

Andi ducked her head, relaxed, and let the kitten go. As usual, Justin knew just the right words to help soothe her hurting heart.

"You have so many good memories with this friend," Justin reminded her. "Christmas is coming. Instead of crying for what can never be, perhaps you could think of a special gift for Riley's going away. Something he will remember you by, like a Christmas good-bye."

Andi pondered but didn't reply.

"What do you say? Come on down for supper and show Riley and his father that a Carter can rejoice with others. You know the verse. 'Rejoice with them that do rejoice and—'"

"'—weep with them that weep,'" Andi finished.

Right now, she was in the weeping mood.

Justin hugged her. "We will all weep with you after Riley has left. But for now, can you rejoice that he's going home to be with his family?"

Andi bit her lip. Did she really want Riley to see her with a red face and puffy eyes and remember her that way?

Of course not!

She untangled herself from Justin's hold and stood up. Carefully, she picked every piece of hay from her hair and clothes. Then she looked her brother full in the face.

"I'll try."

Justin smiled and lifted the lantern. "Good girl."

His words and glowing face warmed Andi through and through. But there was one teensy-weensy problem.

What could she give Riley for a Christmas good-bye?

Chapter Three

A Christmas good-bye gift, Justin said.

It must be something so special that Riley would never, *ever* forget Andi Carter. *Even if he lives to be one hundred*, she thought.

What could she give him? It would take days and days to think of something just right, but Andi did not have days and days. She had only *one* day, Sunday. That was hardly enough time to think of a present for her best friend.

Even if she did think up something, Goodwin's Mercantile was not open on Sunday. No stores in Fresno opened on Sunday, the Lord's Day.

Riley and his father planned on leaving the Circle C ranch bright and early Monday morning. "It's a long train trip back to the Presidio," he'd told the Carter family after supper Saturday evening. "Plus, I have to settle Riley's horse Midnight and my Toby into a freight car."

So soon? Andi had gasped, but only on the inside. After her talk with Justin, she had repeated the Bible verse about rejoicing over and over in her head. Whenever she wanted to cry, she recited that verse.

No tears! When Riley left, she could cry as much as she wanted. Justin had said so. But not now.

After Sunday school, Andi ducked into her room.

She opened her treasure box and dug around inside. Maybe there was something in here that might please Riley and cause him to remember her forever and ever.

She lifted out her favorite treasure, a rattlesnake's rattle Mitch had brought home from the hills a couple of years ago. She shook it.

The *rustle, rustle* of the segments brought a smile to Andi's face. Boy, how she'd scared Melinda's friend Sarah that first awful day of school! When she told Riley about it that afternoon, they had both rolled in the hay, laughing their heads off.

A rattlesnake's rattle might make a good Christmas goodbye. Then she noticed that one of the brittle segments had broken off.

Andi sighed. *No.* Sooner or later, a rattlesnake's rattle would break up and fall apart. She tossed it back inside her special box. Then she poked around to find something extra special, but nothing else struck her fancy.

Riley wouldn't care about the shell necklace from Choo-nook, even though he had been there when the Indian girl gave it to Andi. She shook her head. A necklace would remind Riley of Choo-nook, not Andi.

A wild turkey feather was no good, either. How would a feather remind Riley of his best friend when he was far away in the city?

Andi flung herself on her bed and thought. She couldn't give Riley a kitten. His mother might not let him keep it.

She couldn't send a baby chick or a calf, either.

She glanced at the piggy bank on her bookshelf. There was no use counting her money. What few dimes, pennies, and quarters she found were no good today. Not when the town's stores were closed.

Besides, whatever she bought—a top, a whistle, or a bright-blue bandana—were just *things*. Riley wouldn't find anything special in store-bought toys.

Just then, the Sunday afternoon sunshine shone in through the French doors. Something reflected off a piece of glass on her shelf, catching Andi's eye.

She sat up and took a closer look. Sitting next to her piggy bank, a photograph in a gilded frame rested. The picture showed a girl and a boy, along with their horses.

Andi reached up. Trembling fingers took hold of the picture, and she brought it close to her face.

Just last month, Aunt Rebecca had arrived at the ranch on one of her famous surprise visits. Along with a couple of wide-brimmed hats for Andi and Melinda, she also brought a young man, a photographer.

Andi didn't want to argue with her aunt, so she put on her white dress and the horrible hat. Then she stood stiff as a statue while the fussy photographer hid under his black cloth and snapped her picture.

Later, after Melinda was subjected to the same picture-taking event, Andi came up with an idea—an *excellent* idea. Perhaps the photographer would be willing to take a picture of Andi and Riley and their horses.

Aunt Rebecca hemmed and hawed and frowned, but she finally agreed to make the arrangements.

Andi studied the photograph in her hands. A smile cracked her face. Riley had not been too happy about this idea, but he'd gone along with it. Good ol' Riley! He stood stiffly, clutching his big, black horse's reins, looking like he wished he was anyplace else.

Andi, dressed in white, stood next to Riley, smiling brightly and showing off her young filly.

Andi and Riley. Taffy and Midnight.

Sudden, happy tears swam in Andi's eyes. This was the perfect Christmas good-bye. Riley could not forget Andi if he had her likeness. She quickly found a scrap of tissue paper and tied up the package with a bright-blue ribbon.

When Andi finished, she set the gift on her bedside table. Then she whispered, "I can't wait to see his face!"

Chapter Four

Monday morning dawned clear, but crisp and cold. Winter was without a doubt on the way. Christmas waited just around the corner.

Andi had been up since before dawn. She didn't want to miss Riley's going away, even though the whole family had said good-bye last night in the parlor.

Andi had said good-bye too, but it wasn't the same when she stood with all the grown-ups. She knew Riley felt awkward too.

"Meet me tomorrow morning in the hayloft before you leave," she'd whispered before she went upstairs to bed.

Now, Andi waited on scratchy hay, shivering in the dimly lit, predawn barn.

Meow.

Bella rubbed her head against Andi's legs, purring a happy good morning at this unexpected loft visitor.

Riley's head popped up at the top of the ladder just then. "Hi, Andi!"

Andi nearly jumped out of her skin. "You scared me."

Riley swung into the loft and plopped down next to her. "I was practicing my Indian sneak."

"That was pretty good," Andi admitted.

Riley laughed. "I've got it down *real* good by now."

He sure did. He'd sneaked up on Andi without making a sound.

Riley looked up at the high peak. "Can I swing on the rope one more time?"

Andi shrugged. "Sure."

Riley scrambled to his feet and grabbed the end of the rope Slipping and sliding, he climbed to the top of a large haystack. Then with a whoop, he pushed off and swung in a wide arc over Andi's head.

When he let go, he fell into a pile of hay not far from Andi. "I'm gonna miss this hayloft," he said softly when he'd brushed off the hay and settled himself next to Andi. "I'm gonna miss *you*."

Tears stung Andi's eyes. *Rejoice with them that do rejoice.* "I'm gonna miss you too." Her voice caught. "But I'm glad you can be with your mother and father again."

Riley picked up a piece of hay and twirled it between his fingers. "You have the best ranch in all of California."

"Riley!" Captain Prescott called. "Let's go!"

Riley rose. "Coming, Pa!"

Andi dug her hand into her pocket. It was now or never. "Wait, Riley. I"—she swallowed—"I have something for you. Something so you won't forget me."

Riley laughed. "I'll never forget *you*, Andi. Not ever. You're my best friend."

Andi thrust the tissue-wrapped package into his hands. "This is to make sure you don't." She smiled. "Plus, it's a Christmas present."

Riley yanked the ribbon loose and tore away the tissue paper. "Andi!"

He gasped and looked at her. His hazel eyes were wide and full of surprise. "I—I don't know what to say."

Andi stood up and faced him. "Say 'thank you' and get going before your pa comes looking for you." Then she threw her arms around her friend. "Good-bye, Riley."

"Riley!" His father's voice grew louder. He poked his head into the barn. "Time to go. *Now.*"

Riley gently pulled himself from Andi's tight hug. "Thank you." With the photo clutched in one hand, he scurried down the ladder, waved, and disappeared from Andi's life.

After Riley left, Andi threw herself down into the hay and sobbed her heart out.

Note: Riley Prescott returns to the Carter ranch eight years later (1884) in the Circle C Milestones book, *The Last Ride*.

2. Andi's Christmas Blizzard

Chapter One

December 1877
This story is set three weeks after the events in *Andi to the Rescue*.

"I sure wish it would snow."

Nine-year-old Andi Carter slumped in her chair at the breakfast table and picked at her bowl of oatmeal. It was drenched in white sugar and thick cream, but she couldn't enjoy it. Not today.

Just past the tall French doors that led outside to the patio, the California sun shone down warm and bright. The temperature had dropped last night, but the water in the horse trough didn't freeze.

She was pretty sure the thermometer would hit seventy degrees in the shade.

What kind of Christmas was *that*?

The stories in Andi's school readers revolved around winter, and winter everywhere except California was filled with snow, icicles, and red-cheeked children—mostly boys—flying down hills on their new Christmas sleds.

She plopped her elbows on the table and glared out the window. "Why, oh why, can't it snow, even once?"

"Snow?" Chad scratched his chin and turned to Justin. "How's your memory, big brother? Do you remember the last time it snowed on this ranch?"

Justin pondered. Then he snapped his fingers. "I do remember. I was thirteen. You were twelve. Mitch somehow got his face washed in two inches of snow."

"No, brother Justin," Chad argued. "One inch of snow."

The brothers laughed at this old, well-worn story.

Mitch did not laugh. "You were a couple of bullies. I remember it perfectly. A mean trick to play on a seven-year-old boy, washing his face in the snow like that."

Chad and Justin gave Mitch innocent blue looks. "We? Bullies? We were including you in our romp in the snow."

"I got you back with those dead bugs I collected fro—"

"Never mind." Andi sighed impatiently. She did not want to hear this snow tale one more time. "Why couldn't it snow more than one time in"—she wrinkled her forehead and did the arithmetic—"twelve years?"

Justin winked. "You cipher quite well, honey."

Right now, Andi's favorite and easiest subject was not important. "Don't change the subject,"

Mother smiled. "Your brothers have decided to take today off from ranch work, Andrea. They're heading for the high country to cut down our Christmas tree."

Andi's eyes widened. "Even Justin?"

"Yes, even me. The courts can do without my lawyering for one day." He chuckled. "Would you like to come along?"

Andi dropped her spoon. It landed in her oatmeal with a quiet *splat*. A blob of mush found Andi's cheek, but she ignored the messy spot. "*Me?* Really? But what about—"

She snapped her mouth shut just in time. She did not want the word "school" to fly out of her mouth. There were still three days left before school let out for the holidays.

Worse, Mother was still the substitute teacher while Miss Hall's sprained ankle healed. Would she let her own daughter play hooky from school?

Mother looked at her kindly. "It won't hurt if you miss one day of school. I'm sure the schoolboard won't scold the substitute teacher for allowing a student to have a little fun with her brothers." She turned to Justin. "Am I right?"

Justin, a member of the schoolboard, nodded. "As always, Mother."

"And you will be home in time for supper?"

"Yes, and we'll be as hungry as four bears," Chad replied, grinning. "We're only going high enough to find a bushy fir tree."

"High enough to find some snow," Andi said.

"Of course, Sis," Mitch agreed.

A sudden burst of generosity exploded inside Andi. As much as she wanted to play hooky from school and find snow today, it might be nicer to wait for Melinda.

"Maybe Melinda would like to come with us. She'll be home next week from Miss Whitaker's Academy. I bet she's ready for a nice, long holiday. She's been gone since the fall."

It seemed like an eternity since Andi's fourteen-year-old big sister had left, and she missed her dreadfully.

"That is very kind, Andrea," Mother said, smiling. "But Melinda would probably rather walk in the door and see everything decorated and smelling like Christmas."

"True," Mitch said. "She's not one to tramp around in the wilderness."

Andi clapped her hands. "I am!"

"That's why we invited you to go along this year," Chad reminded her.

"You'd better finish that cereal so you have the energy to help with the tree," Mother suggested.

Andi dug into her now-cold oatmeal and chugged it down so fast that Mother warned her to slow down before she choked.

I'm going to see snow! Her thoughts whirled faster than the top Cory had brought to school last week. Most years Chad and Mitch cut the tree while she was in school. It was a rough trip—too exhausting for little girls.

Not this year, though. "I reckon nine years old is big enough to go on such a snowy adventure," she said to herself. Everyone else had left the table.

A minute later, she pushed back her chair, carried her empty bowl to the kitchen, and flew up the stairs to get ready for the all-day adventure into the mountains.

Andi clomped down the stairs feeling like a grizzly bear dressed for winter. She slid her hand along the banister railing but knew she was too bundled to climb aboard and slide down.

Under her overalls Andi wore a pair of long johns—red flannel underwear—and a flannel shirt Mitch had lent her. She found her red wool coat and hat without any trouble.

Finding mittens was harder. No one needed mittens in California, at least not in the valley.

But Mother helped, and soon Andi was loaded with winter clothes both on her body and in her arms.

She piled the heaping load of outerwear into the wagon bed. Then she laid her snowshoes on top. Funny-looking footwear, but the boys promised they would show her how they worked. They'd better. Snowshoes looked tricky.

Mitch tossed in a saw and a double-bit ax.

"Be extra careful with this," Mother advised. She handed Mitch a wicker basket full of a picnic lunch.

A picnic in December! *Yum!* Andi wriggled with joy. How blessed she was to have this wonderful family. "Do I get to help pick out the tree?"

"Absolutely," Chad replied. He tossed his winter gear into the wagon bed and looked east. The sun had climbed a little higher into the December sky. "Perfect day. No fog, sunny, and crisp."

"And no rain," Andi put in. Rain meant mud. Circle C ranch mud was the sloppiest, gooiest mud in the entire state. Once, Andi lost a new pair of riding boots when the mud oozed up past her knees. The only way to get out of the sucking mud was to slip out of her boots and leave them behind.

What a terrible, muddy day that was!

Chad pointed to the faraway peaks. "You'll see snow, today, little sister. You can count on it." He ruffled Andi's hair and headed for the barn.

Ten minutes later, the bay horses, Jingo and Barney, were hitched up to the wagon. Andi found a couple strings of old bells in the tack room and tied them to the harness.

Jingo shook his mane, and the bells jingled. Perfect!

Andi climbed into the back of the wagon. "Let's go!"

Mother strolled up to the wagon just then. Her arms overflowed with blankets. "You will be warm and cozy if you don't have to sit on that hard wagon bed."

"Thank you, Mother." Andi piled the blankets on the floor of the wagon bed and plopped down to try them out. They felt warm and cozy, all right. *Too* warm and cozy.

Drops of sweat were starting to form at the back of Andi's neck. The sun was so warm that she wanted to peel off her flannel underwear. Maybe she had dressed too warmly too soon.

Justin, Chad, and Mitch were in shirtsleeves.

"Have a lovely time," Mother said. "Hot chili and Luisa's famous cornbread for supper."

Andi's stomach rumbled, even though breakfast had just ended. *Yummy!*

Chad gave the horses a slap with the reins. The wagon jerked, and they were on their way.

Chapter Two

"Jingle bells, jingle bells, jingle all the way . . ."

Andi sang at the top of her lungs, right along with her brothers. The words, mixed with the horses' jingling bells, echoed back from the rolling hills. It was a Christmas song, and Andi knew most of the words.

She sang all the verses she knew and thought the song was over, but then Chad sang another verse in a clear, deep voice.

"A day or two ago,
I thought I'd take a ride,
And soon Miss Fanny Bright
Was seated at my side.

The horse was lean and lank;
Misfortune seemed his lot.
He got into a drifted bank,
And then we got upsot."

"What does upsot mean, Chad?" Andi asked.

"Spilled out of the sleigh," Chad answered. Then he sang the rest of the ballad about a poor young man who was left adrift in the snow when his sleigh overturned.

Andi laughed at all the silly verses.

The morning flew by. Jingo and Barney trotted along until the road became too steep, narrow, and curvy. Then Chad slowed the horses to a walk.

Andi had been too busy singing and watching the hills that seemed to grow larger the higher they went. Then she glanced behind the wagon and gasped. "Look!"

The wagon had left two long, wide lines in a thin dusting of snow. The brown, winter-dead grass pushed up through the snow, but not for long. Ten minutes later, the snow was a few inches deep. Only the tops of the highest grasses could poke through.

An hour later, the world turned sparkling white.

Andi looked up. High overhead, towering ponderosa pines and firs poked the sky. *For sure, I want to do this every year.*

She took a deep breath.

Then she blew tiny puffs of air and watched the clouds of breath float away. "Why is my breath cloudy?" she asked.

Justin turned from his place on the high wagon seat and answered patiently. "Your warm breath is full of tiny water droplets. The cold air can't hold all that water, so when your breath hits the cold air, it condenses, which makes your breath look misty."

Andi didn't know what "condenses" meant, so she just smiled and said "oh." Then she went back to daydreaming of ice castles and snow princesses.

The wagon jerked to a sudden halt in the middle of one of Andi's imaginary stories. She fell backward onto the mound of blankets. "What's wrong?"

"Nothing," Justin said. "The snow is too deep to drive the wagon any farther."

"We'd need a sleigh to keep going," Mitch added. "Look how deep it is."

Andi glanced over the side of the wagon and gasped. "Snow!" She couldn't wait to explore this white fluffiness.

"You haven't seen anything yet," Chad warned. "You'd better bundle up in more clothes."

Andi's brothers jumped down from the wagon and pulled on their coats and heavy gloves.

"I hope you're wearing extra socks inside those boots," Chad said. "From here on, we walk, and it's a long way."

Andi looked with longing at Mother's picnic basket. "Can we eat first?"

Mitch nodded. "Good idea, lil Sis. I'm hungry too."

Andi dug into Mother's tasty roast-beef sandwiches and leftover chocolate cake from last night. She took a sip from her canteen and squealed. Ice-cold lemonade instead of water!

Wouldn't the boys be surprised?

They were, and it wasn't long before they felt refreshed and ready to go after that perfect Christmas tree.

The road soon narrowed to a slight path through the forest. The snow came up past Andi's knees. She trudged behind her brothers, panting. *This is a lot of work.*

She didn't say it out loud. They might not take her next year if she couldn't keep up. So, she lifted her legs higher and kept going.

After what seemed like hours later, Justin held up his hand. "It's time for snowshoes," he said. "We can't keep breaking this path. I'm beat." He pulled Andi up next to him. "So is Andi."

No, I'm not, Andi wanted to argue, but that would not be the truth. Her legs trembled from working so hard.

"That's what you get for spending all your time in a fancy lawyer's office instead of giving Mitch and me a hand on the range," Chad teased. But he and Mitch stopped to latch their snowshoes to their boots.

Justin helped Andi with her snowshoes.

Andi grinned. "I'm glad I can wear them. They're too heavy to carry."

Two minutes later, Andi was *not* glad she could wear her snowshoes. Ker-*plunk!* She tripped over the snowshoes' tips and fell head first into the snow. *Brrr!*

She now knew what it felt like to have her face washed in snow. No wonder Mitch didn't like that old story. The snow was so cold that it burned like fire on her cheeks. "These things are harder to use than I thought they'd be," she said.

"You'll get used to them," Chad told her. "Let's go."

Chad was right. The farther into the forest they hiked, the easier the snowshoes became to use.

So long as Andi made sure she lifted each foot all the way up, the tip did not catch on the snow. Snowshoes were long, heavy, and clumsy, but she made them work.

Chad and Mitch walked fast. Andi couldn't keep up, so Justin stayed behind with her. More often than not, he held her mittened hand and saved her from a dump in the snow.

"Are you doing all right?" Justin asked a few minutes later. He pulled Andi to her feet after another tumble and brushed off the snow.

"What's the hurry?" She panted for breath. "They'll pick out . . . the tree before I can . . . get there."

"Don't worry." Justin smiled. "I promise they'll wait for you."

"Over here!" Chad yelled. His voice echoed, *"over here . . ."*

"Come on, honey," Justin urged. "It's not far now."

Justin was right. Just around the bend of the trail, a beautiful clearing opened up. "Oh, my!" Andi whispered.

Chad grinned. "Yes, sirree. The best spot for trees." He waved his hand across a vast blanket of white. Elk and deer tracks showed everywhere in the deep snow. Tall trees rose high. Young trees stood half-buried under a fresh layer of snow.

"Go 'head and pick out a tree, Andi," Mitch said.

Andi beamed. She wasn't tired anymore. She spent the next half hour looking over the fir trees. One was too bushy. Another was too short. Others showed too much elk and deer damage.

"This one," Andi finally shouted, pointing straight up.

A white fir stood about ten feet tall. It was much taller than Justin, Chad, or Mitch, but it would fit perfectly in Mother's high-ceilinged parlor.

Chad whistled, long and low. "I think you're right, Andi. This tree looks just about perfect."

They boys spent the next fifteen minutes scraping snow from around the base of the tree so they could chop it down.

Finally, Chad grabbed the ax and went to work. "Stay out of the way," he warned Andi.

She scooted halfway across the clearing, just in case.

Soon, a *zing* and a *whack* told Andi the tree was coming down, and in her direction. It hit the ground with a muffled *thunk*. Snow flew up and smacked her cheeks.

"It stings!" she yelled.

Her big brothers kept busy trimming the branches and getting the tree ready to haul back to the wagon. It looked like a heavy tree, but Justin, Chad, and Mitch were strong. They could drag it across the snow with no problem.

After trimming the branches, Mitch found the long rope they'd brought along. The boys started wrapping the tree's branches close to the trunk.

Andi couldn't help with this part of the Christmas tree adventure. She reached down and scooped up a handful of snow. Then she added more snow until she had a perfect ball. She grinned. Snow was a wonder. It made perfect round balls.

What should she do with this marvelous creation? Remembering how cold her face had become in the snow, she was sure snow in other parts of a body would be just as cold.

Andi started toward her brothers. Mitch and Justin were on the far side of the tree, tightening the knots. Chad was closer. He was down on his knees, tying the final knots in his length of the rope. His back was to Andi, and his coat collar lay open.

Perfect!

One step, two steps . . . Andi reached out and yanked his coat collar wide open. The snowball fit perfectly down his neck. She dropped it in and jumped back, ready to flee.

"Yowwie!" Chad's surprised yelp echoed throughout the meadow. He shivered, shook the snow out of his coat the best he could, and spun on Andi. "I'm gonna get you for that." A wicked, teasing smile covered his face.

Heart hammering, Andi ran. Or *tried* to run. She had taken off her snowshoes, and the snow was deep, too deep to outrun Chad and his long legs. Each step made Andi sink deeper.

Chad caught up. "Gotcha!" He scooped Andi up in his arms and headed back toward Justin and Mitch and the tree. They were watching with wide smiles.

"Let me down!" Andi hollered. Panic rose like a flood. What would Chad do? Wash her face in snow like he had washed Mitch's? Suddenly, her innocent joke was not funny. "I won't do it again. I promise!"

"I'm sure you won't," Chad said. "Not after today."

Chad counted, "One, two, three," then he heaved Andi high in the air. She sailed in a wide arc, arms and legs flailing. She shrieked.

Then *splat!* A deep snowdrift rushed up and hit her full in the face. Her scream was cut off. Snow filled her mouth and nose. She couldn't breathe. She couldn't—

Chuckling, Chad plucked her out. "Learned your lesson?"

Andi shook her head, and the snow went flying from her woolen hat. She brushed off her arms and legs then peered into her brother's bright-blue eyes. "Yes, Chad, I learned my lesson. But oh! Could you please do it again? It was so fun flying through the air." She pointed to the snowdrift. "With a soft landing, even though it's cold."

Chad stared at her, mouth agape. Then he threw back his head and howled his laughter. He tossed her twice more then said it was time to go.

Andi and her brothers strapped on their snowshoes and began the long hike back to the wagon. The boys took turns hauling the giant tree down the trail. They also cut spruce and cedar boughs along the way for household decorations.

Andi yawned. Playing in the snow had worn her out. Her steps came slower and slower. Justin tugged her hand. "I know you're tired, but you have to keep up."

Fearing she might be left home next Christmas spurred Andi on. It felt late. Was it suppertime already? The sun should have been bright, though it was not very high in the sky. The trees blocked the light, but it sure seemed dark right now.

Andi glanced behind her shoulder. Her snowy shadow no longer showed on the trail. She looked up. The whole sky had turned overcast and gray. "Umm, is it going to snow? I hope so."

This was something Andi wanted to see. Snow falling from the sky. A few weeks ago, when Mother and Andi had been held captive in a cabin up in the foothills, she had seen snowflakes.

Those few snowflakes had melted fast. Before she could enjoy their beauty, the flakes had turned back into drizzly rain.

But now? Maybe thousands and thousands of tiny, delicate snowflakes would fall from the sky. *Oh, please! Let it snow!*

Andi's brothers stopped short. They looked surprised. They had been so busy hauling the tree back to the wagon that they had not glanced up at the sky.

They did so now, then they looked at each other. "Uh-oh."

Andi's stomach turned over at their worried expressions.

"A storm's headed our way," Chad said. "It's—"

A sudden, icy wind snatched away the rest of Chad's words. The wind whipped down the path and tore through Andi's coat like a cold knife.

She gasped.

Chapter Three

"We gotta go!" Mitch yelled. "C'mon! Hurry!" He took off down the path.

"Go where?" Andi wanted to know. "Why?"

Nobody heard her questions over the howling wind.

Justin and Chad dropped the tree. Justin grabbed Andi and ripped the snowshoes from her feet. Then he picked her up and started running. Andi heard him huff and puff.

The wind slammed against them, driving hard little icicles into their backs. Snow blew everywhere, slamming into Andi's face. It felt like sharp needles. *Ouch!*

Then a terrible thought struck her. They were leaving their beautiful Christmas tree behind, in the middle of the trail. "What about our Christmas tree?" she shouted.

Justin shook his head and didn't answer. Clearly, he needed all of his breath for running.

The wind carried them down the path at a fast run. So much snow blew that Andi could barely see the fir trees. Just ahead, Chad and Mitch looked like dark, fuzzy shapes.

A minute later, Chad stopped. He reached out his arms for Andi. Justin handed her over, panting. He nodded his thanks.

Chad took off at a lumbering run. Andi held onto his neck.

Nobody spoke. Nobody told Andi where they were going. She shivered and ducked her head against Chad's chest. "I'm cold," she yelled between chattering teeth.

"I . . . know," Chad hollered back. He was panting.

A minute later, Andi saw the dark outlines of the wagon and the two horses.

Mitch and Justin were already there. They grabbed the bridles and urged the horses off the trail, deeper into the woods. The trees would give them some protection.

Chad and Andi nearly blew into the wagon. He dropped her on the forest side, where the wind wasn't blowing as hard. Andi clamped her jaw shut against the cold. Not even all of her layers of outerwear could keep her from shivering.

Cold fear clutched her heart. How would they get warm?

The horses and wagon stood in a thicket of close-growing young trees. The horses whinnied. They didn't like the scratchy branches one bit.

Chad calmed them down and set the wagon brake. Then he made his way over to Justin. "It's the best shelter I can find for now," he hollered over the blizzard's whipping wind.

Justin pulled Andi close to his face. "Listen to me. I have to help make some kind of shelter. I'm putting you in the back of the wagon. Cover up with the blankets and stay put. Do you understand?"

Andi nodded. Justin lifted her and dropped her into the wagon bed. Scared out of her wits—and colder than ever—she burrowed under the blankets.

The coverings didn't help much, but at least the wind was blocked a little. An icy ache entered her belly. Her head hurt from clenching her jaw, and she shivered.

Darkness pressed down on Andi where she cowered under the blankets. The wind howled, and snowflakes rattled against the wagon's sides. They sounded like thousands and thousands of tiny pebbles. *This snow is no fun. It must be a blizzard.*

A scary thought stabbed her freezing thoughts. What if Justin, Chad, and Mitch had been blown away in the blizzard? What if she was left out here all alone? What if—

A sudden bump from underneath the wagon jolted Andi from her scary *what ifs*. What were her brothers doing under the wagon? *Don't leave me alone!*

Time crawled. Then without warning, her blankets flew off. Stinging snow struck Andi's face.

"Come on!" Chad looked half frozen. He yanked Andi out of the wagon.

"Where are we going?"

Chad didn't answer. He dropped to his knees and shoved Andi under the wagon.

Instantly, the wind died away. It was still cold, but this was much better. Andi sat up and looked around.

Except for the hole Chad had pushed her through, a wall of snow filled all four sides from the ground up to the wagon bed. The boys were busy hauling snow to pack around the wagon.

Under the wagon, fir branches were piled thickly on top of the snowy ground. Mitch took one of the blankets and laid it over the evergreens.

Andi scooted out of the way and let him work.

Justin, Chad, and Mitch worked fast, but the light was nearly gone by the time they crawled under the wagon. They were breathing hard and shivering.

Justin plugged the entry hole and leaned back against the wagon wheel. "Now, we wait."

Outside, the snow piled up and the blizzard raged, but under the wagon, Andi could not hear the worst of it. But what about the horses? "Will Barney and Jingo be all right?"

"They're sheltered by the wagon and the trees," Chad said. "It won't be long before we feel warmer too."

"C-can you build a f-fire?" Andi's teeth chattered. "I'm awfully c-cold."

Chad sighed. "No, little sister. Not unless you want to burn the roof over our heads."

A hot flush crept up Andi's cheeks. *What a silly idea!*

"Come here," Justin said. "I'll wrap you up in a blanket."

Andi felt her way across the prickly blanket and into Justin's arms. A minute later she found herself wrapped up tighter than a mummy.

Justin's gloved hands were trembling with cold, but he kept his voice cheerful. "You'll be warm in a jiffy."

I don't think I will ever be warm again, Andi thought.

"Did anybody remember to grab the picnic basket?" Mitch asked.

Justin and Chad shook their heads.

"Anybody feel like going after it?"

Nobody volunteered.

For a long time nobody spoke. Slowly, Andi's shivering grew less. So did Justin's. He slouched against the wagon wheel and snuggled Andi close.

"Is it suppertime yet?" Andi finally asked.

"Probably," Mitch answered from a dark corner. The wind moaned. "I think we're in for a long night."

"With the four of us in this snug little igloo, we'll be fine," Justin said. "Bless Mother for remembering to throw in the blankets this morning. We'll keep close together to conserve warmth. The storm will be over soon."

Justin's cheerful words were met with silence.

Andi did not like the silence. It was too dark and too quiet, except for that awful, howling wind. "Tell me a story."

Chad groaned. Justin sighed. Mitch let out a big breath. But one by one, her brothers told stories about when they were little boys on the ranch.

Andi's eyelids drooped. Wrapped in Justin's arms, she slowly began to feel warm.

She drifted off to sleep.

Chapter Four

Murmuring voices and a scraping sound woke Andi with a start. *Where am I?* She felt stiff and cold, but at least her shivering had stopped.

Andi opened her eyes. Dim light was trickling through the snowy walls. It was bright enough to see Chad and Mitch. They were digging in the snow.

"What are you doing?" she croaked. Her mouth felt full of cotton.

Neither brother answered. They were too busy.

"The wind died down during the last hour," Justin told her. "We think the storm has passed."

"What time is it?"

"Probably a little past sunup."

Andi frowned. "Don't you have your pocket watch?"

"I don't carry Father's pocket watch with me on tree-cutting expeditions. I wouldn't want it to get broken."

Nobody knew the time. Nobody seemed to care.

Andi's stomach always did an excellent job of telling time. Right now, it told her it was time for breakfast.

Andi felt wiggly too. She wasn't sure how to tell Justin that she needed to find a tree or a bush as soon as possible. Finally, she whispered in his ear.

"It won't be long now," he said. "Look."

Andi turned toward one snowy wall.

Chad and Mitch were digging a tunnel through the wall. Andi watched as they wriggled through the snow to the outside world.

First Mitch, then Chad disappeared.

A moment later, Mitch poked his head in. "It's beautiful out here. Come and see."

Andi crawled into a tunnel first. It was not a tight fit and she hurried as fast as she could. An enormous snowdrift had blown against the wagon during the night.

Finally, Andi saw bright, white light ahead. Sunlight! Mitch took hold of her arms and pulled her the rest of the way.

The morning was crisp and sunny. A thousand sparkly diamonds danced on the snow. Andi squinted.

Justin squirmed his way out from the snow tunnel and stood up. He stretched, stomped, and looked around. Then he motioned Andi to his side. "Over there." He pointed to a clump of bushes where the snow was not so deep. "Be quick about it."

Andi hurried.

When she returned to the wagon, Justin, Chad, and Mitch were scraping snow from Jingo's and Barney's backs. The horses whinnied their unhappiness, but they'd made it safely through the night. The trees gave them protection, and the wagon had been a good windbreak, but they looked ready to go home.

I'm ready too, Andi thought.

She glanced at the wagon. Snow had filled the wagon box clear up past the sides. Somewhere under there lay the remains of their picnic lunch. It would take a long time to shovel the snow away.

Chad looked at Andi from where he was working with the

horses. "I want you to crawl back under the wagon and drag out the blankets."

A blanket sounded like a good idea, so Andi squeezed back into the little hidey hole, which felt warm and cozy. It smelled like Christmas.

It took two trips to drag the heavy, woolen blankets out into the daylight. Andi shook them free of snow and fir needles and laid them aside.

The boys were whispering to each other.

"What's the matter?" Andi asked. "Are you thinking of going back for our Christmas tree?" She shaded her eyes and looked up the trail. Their perfect tree had been dropped somewhere back there. The snow was so deep that in her heart, she knew her brothers could not go back for it.

She wasn't surprised when Mitch said, "I'm afraid not."

"That tree is snowed in," Justin added. "It will stay there until the spring thaw."

Tears welled up but Andi blinked them back. She could not do anything about their perfect tree. Nobody could. It was buried, maybe forever.

"You wanted to see snow, Andi." Mitch spread his arms wide. "I reckon you've seen enough snow to last you many, many years. Not many people experience a blizzard."

True, Andi thought. Snow *was* beautiful, but a blizzard was scary. Then she sighed. "We didn't get a Christmas tree."

Justin lifted Andi's chin. "Don't worry, honey, we'll cut a tree. It might not be an elegant white fir, but it'll be pretty. Right now, though, we need to head home. Mother is probably worried about us."

Andi bit her lip. Justin was right. Mother should not worry. She had probably worried all night.

Maybe she let the children out of school so she could wait at home for us. Then she thought, *No school today!* Maybe blizzards were not so bad, after all.

"How are you going to get the wagon out of that snowdrift?" Andi asked. Even if they managed it, wheels were no good in deep snow. "We need a sleigh."

"You're right," Chad said. "But we don't have one, so we'll make do with the next best thing." He rigged the harnesses up on Barney and Jingo. "I'm not leaving good leather harnesses out here for the scavengers to steal."

Andi glanced from the wagon to Chad and then to Jingo and Barney. A light came on inside her cold, tired mind. "We're going to ride the horses home."

Chad nodded. "Which one do you want to ride?"

"Jingo," Andi answered. She hurried over and stroked his nose. "I'm glad you're all right."

Jingo blew a hot, horsey breath into Andi's face.

Just then, Mitch came around from the other side of the wagon. He was covered with snow from head to toe.

"I found the ax." He held it up. "We'll chop down a tree on our way home, where the snow isn't so deep."

Andi beamed. They might not bring home the perfect tree, but at least they would bring home a *Christmas* tree.

It took most of the morning to ride down from the mountains. Barney had no trouble dragging the tree Mitch cut down. It was lighter than a sleigh and lighter than a wagon.

The horses trotted side by side. Justin and Andi rode Jingo. Chad and Mitch rode Barney. Their hooves clomped through the deep snow as easily as if they were trotting along J Street.

Only a trace of snow remained in the foothills. The tree Mitch cut down stayed behind. They would go back for it with the buckboard, but now it was more important to get home.

There wasn't a flake of snow in the valley. Just mud.

Andi pushed away the blanket she'd wrapped around her shoulders. It was hard to imagine how much snow she had left a few hours ago.

A few miles from the ranch house Chad whistled and waved. "It looks like Mother stayed home and rounded up a search party."

"Mother is riding with them," Andi yelled. "Mother!"

Justin nudged Jingo into a lope. Soon, the search party gathered around Andi and her brothers.

"Thank God, you're safe," Mother prayed out loud.

Andi slid off Jingo, and Mother slid off Misty. She threw her arms around Andi. Then she looked up at Justin.

"Blizzard," he said.

Mother's face turned pale. "I saw the clouds over the mountains last night. The weather came up so fast. We had a terrible rain and windstorm." She squeezed Andi tight. "I was praying hard."

"Oh, Mother!" Andi said. "We found the perfect tree, but we had to leave it behind . . . and the boys made a snow igloo out of the wagon and snow . . . and they dug a tunnel to get out this morning . . . and—"

"Hush now." She smiled. "You can tell me all about it later."

She laid her gloved hand on Andi's shoulder. "Luisa has hotcakes, crispy bacon, and hot coffee for breakfast," Mother told her tired-looking sons. "And hot chocolate for Andrea."

Mmm! Andi scrambled up on Misty with Mother, and they all headed home.

It wasn't a bad-looking Douglas fir tree, at least not after everybody added the decorations: cookies, popcorn strings, candles, and fancy glass ornaments.

The tree was so full of decorations that nobody could see the broken-off branches. Being dragged through the snow had not done the Christmas tree any good.

Melinda saw the tree a week later and loved it. She liked the story of how they had gotten the tree even better. Her eyes sparkled at the retelling. "Oh, Andi," she exclaimed, "weren't you scared and cold?"

"Oh, yes," Andi said, "but there's not many who can say they lived through a blizzard. That's what Chad told me."

When the family gathered around the piano for their carol singing, Melinda started right in. Most of the time they sang songs like "Hark! The Herald Angels Sing" and "Silent Night."

This year, though, Melinda began the caroling with "Dashing through the snow . . ."

Andi sang along with *all* the verses, especially the ones about the poor fellow who'd been dumped in a snowdrift.

She knew exactly how he felt.

3. Andi's Interrupted Christmas

Chapter One

Early December 1878

Ten-year-old Andi Carter bounded into the ranch house after school one December afternoon. She flew straight into her mother's arms. "This is going to be the best Christmas ever! Guess why."

Big brother Chad walked in just then. "Because it might snow for once?" He took a bite of his apple and grinned.

Andi rolled her eyes. "That would be nice, but no. It's something *much* better than snow."

Mother smiled. "I see you're bursting with news."

"Spill it before you explode," Chad said.

Andi untangled herself from Mother's embrace. She stepped back and stood up tall. "Out of all the girls—even pretty Mary Ellen Meyers and ladylike Priscilla Johnson—Miss Hall chose *me*."

She bounced up and down on her tiptoes. "Isn't that the most exciting news you ever heard?"

"Depends on what she chose you for," Chad said. "To clean the chalk boards? I wouldn't consider *that* much of an honor."

"Chad, please." Mother waved his teasing away. "Let her finish."

"I'm to play the part of Mary during the Christmas pageant at school on Christmas Eve."

Mother smiled. "That's wonderful, sweetheart."

"I was sure Mary Ellen would get the part," And said. "On account of her name is *Mary*. And how pretty she is. Or Priscilla, since she was Mary last year and knows the part." Andi twirled. "But Miss Hall chose *me*."

Andi could not believe her good fortune. Last year she had played a shepherd boy. Her head covering fell off during the pageant, and her dark, tangled hair tumbled down, exposing her as a shepherd *girl*. Oh, the shame!

The year before that Andi had played an angel—one of many. Johnny Wilson, the classroom bully, said they put all the leftover kids in the angel choir.

Leftover didn't sound very nice. But then, Johnny was never nice. He always played the part of King Herod. Johnny came by the king's meanness naturally.

"The older girls usually play Jesus' mother," Andi said. "Remember when Melinda played Mary?"

Mother nodded.

Andi sighed. "I've always wanted to play the part of Mary, but it never happens. Another girl always gets to."

Perhaps Miss Hall wanted only ladylike children to play such an important role. Andi knew *she* would never be ladylike enough to be Mary . . . until this year.

"When Miss Hall said, 'Andrea Carter will be Mary this year,' I almost fell out of my seat," Andi said breathlessly. "I was so surprised!"

Chad looked surprised too.

"Congratulations," Mother said. "It is an honor to portray the mother of our Lord. I know you will do your best."

"I sure will!" Andi promised. "I'll memorize every line word-perfect."

"Who will be playing the devoted Joseph?" Chad's blue eyes teased.

"Cory," she admitted. Her cheeks grew warm. "But he's better than one of the older boys. They begged Miss Hall not to have to play any parts this year. They said they're too old. They would rather haul in the hay and the animals for the backgrounds." *Thank goodness!*

Andi would simply curl up and die if she was matched with fourteen-year-old Frank Allen or Seth Atkins. She might get teased about Cory playing Joseph, but at least she could look him in the face while she held Baby Jesus and not blush. *Speaking of Baby Jesus . . .*

"Guess what else, Mother? Mrs. Samuelson is letting me hold her little Richard. He's one month old and perfect for the Baby. She says he sleeps all the time."

Andi let out a happy sigh. "I will never forget this Christmas, not for as long as I live."

She threw her arms around Mother once more, let Chad ruffle her hair, and flew up the stairs to share the good news with her big sister Melinda.

Chapter Two

The next two weeks flew by quicker than a wildfire. Besides keeping up with her schoolwork, Andi had to learn her lines. She had more lines than anybody else in the pageant.

Andi was so happy to be playing Mary that she didn't care how many lines she must learn. She whipped through her homework so she could practice her part.

The short and easy lines came first, when the angel Gabriel visited Mary. "Behold, the handmaiden of the Lord," she practiced over and over again.

There were a lot more lines to learn for the scene when Mary visited her cousin Elizabeth. A *lot* more.

"Once I get through Mary's song of praise, I won't have to say anything more," Andi said at supper one night.

"Why not?" Big brother Mitch asked.

"During the manger scene, Miss Hall says I just need to gaze down at Baby Jesus and act . . . well . . . her exact words were 'blessed and serene.'"

"I look forward to seeing how you pull *that* part off," Chad said.

Chuckles rippled around the table. Even Mother and Andi's oldest brother Justin were smiling.

Andi ducked her head. *That will be harder than learning my lines.*

Andi practiced her lines to Justin on the way home from school every day for the next two weeks.

"I can nearly recite the lines myself," he said. "You sure are giving this your all."

"I'm going to be the best Mary ever," Andi told him. "I want to make Miss Hall glad she chose me."

When the buggy came to a stop in the yard, Andi leaped out and ran into the house. She flew up the stairs to her sister's room. "Melinda, I'm home!"

Melinda had agreed to help Andi learn her lines. She opened the Bible and found the spot. "I'm ready."

"Don't you remember lines from your own part?"

Melinda shook her head. "A few, but I want to make sure you get it right."

Andi smiled. "Good idea." She took a breath. "My soul doth magnify the Lord, and"—she gulped—"and my spirit hath rejoiced in God my Savior." She paused.

"Well, go on," Melinda said.

"I'm trying to." Andi took another breath. "For he hath . . . hath . . ." She sighed. "Oh, dirty rats! This part always stumps me. It's like a bump in the road. Once I pass it, I can finish."

Melinda frowned. "For one thing, Andi, I can tell you that Mary would never say *dirty rats*."

True. Andi bit her lip. Losing her temper was not a good way to practice being blessed and serene. And she wanted to be, so very much!

"The next word is *regarded*," Melinda said. "'For he hath regarded the low estate of his—"

"His handmaiden!" Andi cut in. "I can do it now." The verses rolled off her tongue, one after the other, with only a few more pauses for help.

Melinda grinned. "You're doing much better. By the time Christmas Eve arrives, you'll know your lines perfectly." She held up a piece of cloth. "Mother said I could stitch your outfit. Shall we try it on?"

Andi fingered the soft blue wool. It matched her eyes perfectly. What a beautiful robe it would make. And the long, white, lace-edged scarf Melinda had borrowed from the top of her dresser made a perfect head covering.

Surely, wearing such a lovely costume would help Andi remember to behave like a blessed and serene mother!

At least she hoped it would . . .

"Johnny Wilson, stop that horseplay this instant and stand still."

Miss Hall was riled up, no two ways about it.

Andi knew why. Every time the teacher's back was turned, King Herod started a riot. He got the shepherds and the angels to go after each other.

The girl angels shrieked when the boy shepherds whacked them with their makeshift staffs.

"For unto you is born this day in the city of David!" Little Julianna Ross shrieked to be heard above the racket.

Toby Wright bumped into the little angel.

Julianna shoved him away and yelled louder. *"For unto you is born this day—"*

Toby fell into Mercy Thompson. They hit the floor with a loud *thump*. Mercy wailed.

"For unto you is born—"

"Oh, hush, would you?" Johnny yelled at Julianna. "Your

screechy voice is burning my ears."

Julianna burst into tears.

"Children!"

Miss Hall waded into the commotion and sorted everybody out. When they quieted down, she brushed a strand of hair from her forehead and nodded at Julianna.

"Start over, please, Julianna. From the beginning." She sighed. "Remember, dear. Angels do not shriek their message. They announce it in a loud and happy voice."

Andi held a beat-up ragdoll in her arms and listened to Julianna announce Baby Jesus' birth. The doll looked nothing like Baby Jesus—or even like baby Richard. But it would have to do for now.

There were ten more days to go until the pageant, but today Andi knew her lines perfectly. Better yet, she could say them with feeling, as if she really was Mary.

Mary, who had seen a real, live angel. Mary, whom God had chosen to be the mother of the Savior.

Even Miss Hall was pleased. She'd smiled at Andi during practice yesterday and praised her. "Such feeling, Andrea! Very good."

But today, Andi didn't want to put feeling into her words. She didn't want to say her lines at all.

She wanted to go home. She felt strange—

"Andrea, did you hear me?"

Andi's head snapped up. "No, ma'am. I'm sorry."

"Let's hear Mary's Song now, if you please."

Andi set the ragdoll down and crossed the room. She looked at Susannah Warner, who was playing the part of Elizabeth. She had a lot of lines too.

"Blessed art thou among women," Susannah began.

Andi barely heard the long speech. Her head spun, and her tongue felt fuzzy. She stared at Susannah and wished she were anyplace else.

"And blessed is she that believed . . ." Susannah recited. She droned on and on.

Susannah's words ran together in Andi's head. She barely heard her . . . and missed her cue.

"My soul doth magnify the Lord," Miss Hall said.

Andi blinked and tried to remember what came next. When she realized she had ten long verses to recite before she could sit down, she recited them as fast as she could. Then she sank down in her place beside Cory to wait for the manger scene.

"Goodness gracious, Andrea!" Miss Hall frowned. "What's come over you? You must show more feeling." She clucked her tongue. "I want you to try it again after the manger scene."

I don't want to, Andi thought with a heavy sigh.

She had felt poorly ever since Justin had dropped her off at school that morning. The day had crawled by. The afternoon practice was crawling even slower.

Andi's cheeks felt flushed. Her throat hurt.

I want to go home.

When the angels finished their lines and brushed by Andi on their way back to "heaven," she shivered. They'd stirred up a draft.

A wave of dizziness suddenly washed over Andi. She clutched the doll and bent over to steady herself.

"Let us now go even unto Bethlehem . . ."

Andi barely heard the shepherds.

"You feelin' all right?" Cory whispered.

Andi nodded. "Just tired." She glanced at the clock. "It's

almost four o'clock."

Maybe she'd feel better when she crawled into the buggy. She could lean against Justin on the ride home.

"Mary and Joseph!" Miss Hall clapped her hands. "Quickly, now. School's nearly out. Come up here so the shepherds can visit the manger."

Cory shot up and grabbed the sturdy oak branch he was using for a staff. When Andi didn't move, he reached down and yanked her arm. "Come on. Miss Hall means business."

"Hurry, Andrea," Miss Hall said. "After the manger scene, you will need to go over your lines with Susannah again."

Andi rose and squinted at Cory through bleary eyes. He seemed to be spinning. *Or I'm spinning.*

She swallowed. Her throat burned. The world spun faster. "I want my mother." Andi closed her eyes and collapsed to the floor with a noisy *thunk*.

Chapter Three

Andi did not get her wish.

When she opened her eyes, it was not Mother but Justin who was lifting her up in his arms. His face was pale, and his eyebrows were scrunched up in a worried frown.

"What's the matter, honey?" he asked softly. "How do you feel?"

Hot tears gathered behind Andi's eyelids. She blinked.

A tear dribbled down the side of her face and into her ear "I'm hot." She shivered. "No, I'm cold. I'm—" She broke off and whimpered. "I want to go home. I want Mother."

"All in good time," Justin said. "But first we need to make a call on Dr. Weaver. You're burning up." He straightened and lifted Andi higher. "It won't take long."

Andi's feet dangled. She snuggled her head against Justin's chest and tried to make sense of where she was.

"I do hope it's nothing serious, Justin."

Hearing Miss Hall's worried voice made everything click. School. The pageant practice.

Andi moaned. *I swooned, just like a weak, silly young lady.*

A worse thought followed. *In front of everybody!* She lifted her head, horrified that she might see her schoolmates laughing at her.

The classroom was empty. Miss Hall must have dismissed school and shooed the students out the door while Andi was unconscious. She let out a shallow breath of relief.

"If you could find Andi's cloak please?" Justin was saying. "We need to be on our way."

Miss Hall nodded. "Of course. Come with me."

Justin's steps lulled Andi into a doze. She barely noticed when Miss Hall and Justin wrapped her up in her outerwear.

"Use my shawl to cover her head," Miss Hall said. "It's pouring rivers outdoors."

Andi fingered the wooly garment. It smelled like the classroom. *Ugh.* But she was too tired and too miserable to yank it from her face.

Justin mumbled his thanks, tightened his arms around Andi, and hurried from the schoolroom.

Andi's world blurred into the sounds of splashing hoof

beats, pattering rain, and Justin's footsteps. She felt herself heaved to and fro. Her throat burned. It was worse than any scratchy throat she had ever had.

A slamming door and the doctor's cheerful voice woke her completely. Dr. Weaver helped Andi sit up. He peered into her eyes. He looked down her throat and frowned. "Under your tongue, missy," he instructed.

A cold thermometer poked into her mouth.

A few minutes later, he checked the thermometer and let her lie down. "Rest easy, Andrea, while I talk to Justin."

Andi closed her eyes but kept her ears wide open.

"I'll wait for the rash to show up before I make my final diagnosis," Dr. Weaver said. "But offhand I'd say she's got herself a case of scarlet fever."

Justin squeezed Andi's hand. "How bad?"

"I can't say for sure," Dr. Weaver replied. "You need to bundle her up and whisk her home as fast as your buggy can carry you. She'll need careful nursing, but I can't keep her here. Your mother would have my hide."

Justin chuckled. It was the first happy sound Andi had heard this afternoon. "You're right about that."

Dr. Weaver did not laugh. "I reckon I'd best get ready for another round of this wretched illness." He let out a deep sigh. "We already had our fill of it last spring."

Andi's mind cleared in an instant. *Scarlet fever?* She shivered. A scarlet fever epidemic had sent Andi to Aunt Rebecca's last May. San Francisco was a safe place when the rest of the valley was suffering.

Scarlet fever? Oh, please, no!

Cory had come down with it. So had Andi's other town friends. Even big brother Mitch had caught it.

Had they felt this awful? She hurt all over.

Justin fumbled with Andi's cloak. "Time to go."

Andi opened her eyes. "Do I have scarlet—"

"Shh." Justin accepted a woolen blanket and a sack of licorice lozenges the doctor held out. "Thanks."

"The lozenges, along with ice chips, will help soothe her throat," Dr. Weaver said. "But she'll have to fight off the fever herself. There's no quick cure."

Justin's jaw clenched. "I know."

He wrapped Andi up like a caterpillar in a cocoon, hiked her up in his arms, and turned to go.

Dr. Weaver opened the door. "I'll drop by the ranch tomorrow to check on her." He laid a gentle hand on Andi's forehead and smiled. "You rest quietly, do what your mother tells you, drink lots of tea, and suck on the lozenges."

"Do I really have scarlet fever?" Andi croaked.

The doctor winked. "Yes, I'm pretty sure you do. But you'll be fine in a couple of weeks."

A couple of weeks? Andi's heart leaped to her sore throat, making it feel tighter than ever. Her eyes were too dry for tears, but they stung anyway. "I can't be sick. Not now. I'm Mary in the pageant and—"

"Hush, my dear," Dr. Weaver scolded her softly. "Don't irritate your sore throat with talking. And don't excite yourself. You'll only make your illness worse."

How could she make herself any sicker than she already felt? Andi wanted to argue with Dr. Weaver. She wanted to beg him to give her medicine that would make her well by tomorrow.

I have to go to school. I must be there for the practice.

By the time she gathered her woozy wits to form the

words, Justin had bundled her out the door and into the covered buggy. He climbed in beside her and slapped the reins over Pal's back. The horse leaped into a trot.

Andi remembered no more.

Chapter Four

It took Andi less than a day to figure out that scarlet fever was nothing like a cold . . . or chicken pox . . . or even influenza.

None of those illnesses set her throat on fire or made her see wild horses racing around her room. The horses snorted and reared, and Andi couldn't get away.

The next minute, the horses galloped far away down a dark tunnel that turned into the size of a pinprick. A second later, the pinprick swelled to a gigantic horse's head, which opened its mouth and—

"Mother!" Andi clutched the sheets and rolled her head from side to side. "Make them go away."

Mother's quiet voice whispered "there, there." She laid a cold, damp cloth on Andi's forehead.

Andi opened her eyes. The light of a low-burning lamp shone from her nightstand. Mother sat beside her.

"Oh, Mother!" Andi told her about the horses. "They were all around me," she finished with a sob.

"Shh," Mother said. "You're delirious." She stood up.

Andi grasped her hand. "Don't go!"

"I'm only going to ask Mitch to break off more ice chunks from the block in the icebox. I'll be right back."

She bent down and brushed Andi's sweat-soaked hair from her face. "You'll feel better in the morning."

But Andi did not feel better in the morning. She felt worse than ever.

Dr. Weaver checked her neck and face then gently rolled her over and peeked at her back. "Yes, it's scarlet fever, all right. There's no mistaking this rash."

He looked up at Mother. "Two more cases broke out during the night. I hope that's as far as it goes, but one can never be sure."

He rose and shook his head. "So far, it looks like Andrea's case is pretty mild. Not like what we saw last spring when we lost—"

Mother cleared her throat, and the doctor broke off.

Andi knew what he was going to say. *When we lost some of the youngest children.* They had died.

"Andrea's a strong girl." He grinned and patted her knee. "You'll beat this thing."

"Not in time for the pageant," Andi croaked.

She winced. It hurt too much to talk. Even if the doctor and Mother allowed her to go, Andi would never be able to say her lines. Ice chips numbed her throat for a minute, but the licorice lozenges did nothing.

After Dr. Weaver left, Andi slept. The frightening vision of the horses came and went. She remembered nothing but ice chips, cold cloths, fresh sheets, and lukewarm, *awful* tea.

Andi wondered if she would ever feel well again.

Andi opened her eyes. The winter sun had risen and was shining through the French doors of her balcony. *How long have I been lying here?* It felt like days and days.

Her heart skipped a beat. Had Christmas come and gone? *Did I miss it?*

In the wingback chair next to the bed, her brother Mitch lay snoring. His head was thrown back over the top edge, and one leg hung over the chair's arm. A blanket lay crumpled on the floor. He looked uncomfortable.

"Mitch?" Andi whispered. Her throat still burned, but she knew without taking her temperature that her fever was gone.

"Huh? What?" Mitch jerked awake and slammed his feet to the floor. Jumping up, he closed the distance between the chair and Andi's bed. "Your fever broke."

His face split into a wide grin, and he wagged his finger at her. "You had us mighty worried, Sis. You were fighting battles in your head." He whistled. "One hundred and four. We've been praying day and night for your fever to break."

Is that what being delirious meant? Fighting dream battles that seemed so real they scared her half to death? She smiled weakly. "Am I cured?"

Mother walked in just then. "Absolutely not." She glided across the room. "But thank the good Lord, the worst is over."

She kissed Andi's cheek. "You've been a very sick little girl these past four days, and you won't be out of the woods for at least another week—possibly two."

Only four days had passed. Andi's heart skipped a beat in joy. *I haven't missed the Christmas pageant!*

Andi threw back her covers and sat up. "I've got to go to school this morning," she said. "If I don't, Miss Hall will choose somebody else to be Mary."

She swallowed past the burning lump in her throat, stood up . . . and fell like a stone.

Mother and Mitch caught her halfway to the floor.

"The infection has sapped your strength," Mother said. She guided Andi back into bed, propped her head against two fluffy pillows, and gave her a firm look.

"I may allow you up long enough to use the chamber pot, but you will stay in bed until this"—she slid Andi's nightgown sleeve past her elbow—"is completely gone."

Andi stared at the bumpy, red rash. "Will I be well enough by Christmas Eve to be in the pageant?"

"I'm afraid not. It's next Wednesday, only six days from now."

Andi opened her mouth to protest, but Mother shook her head.

"Your sore throat will disappear in a day or two, and the rash will be gone by Christmas, but you will still be too weak to go anywhere."

"Please?" Andi whispered. Unwanted tears filled her eyes. She couldn't miss the pageant!

"I'll tie her down or sit on her if you need me to, Mother." Mitch gave Andi the same look Mother had given her a minute ago. "We've seen for ourselves what happens when someone gets up too soon after being ill with this thing."

Mother sat down on the bed and stroked Andi's hair.

"It happened to one of our ranch hands many years ago," she said. "He went back to work too soon and well, he got sicker, and that time he didn't recover."

Andi's mouth dropped open.

"A Christmas pageant is not worth losing you, sweetheart," Mother said. "You will stay in bed for at least another few days.

Then we will see about letting you up to join the family for Christmas Day."

"Yes, Mother." Andi suddenly felt tired. Talking with her family had drained her. She slumped against the pillow and closed her eyes. "I'm sleepy."

A few minutes later, she opened her eyes. Mitch and Mother had left the room. Andi rolled over and let her unshed tears trickle down her cheeks. There would be no Christmas pageant for her this year.

Maybe no Christmas either.

Chapter Five

Andi woke from an afternoon nap four days later to find Justin sitting in the chair next to her bed.

He smiled. "You look better every day." He held out a plate of sugar cookies and a cup of steaming chocolate. "Luisa fixed you a Christmas treat. I wanted to talk to you, so I offered to bring it upstairs."

Andi scooted up against the headboard. For the first time in the week since she'd fallen ill, she felt hungry.

"The cocoa is still warm," Justin said.

Andi eagerly accepted the plate on her lap and bit into the crispy, sugary treat. Her mouth exploded in delight. When she swallowed the hot chocolate, her throat no longer burned.

"*Mmm*." She sighed. "Tell Luisa thank you."

"I will," Justin said.

He helped himself to a cookie and leaned back in his chair. "I have some school news I thought you might like to hear," he said, taking a bite.

Andi stopped chewing. There were only two more days until the pageant. "I don't want to hear the news that Priscilla Johnson took my part as Mary."

Justin chuckled. "I wouldn't ruin your Christmas by telling you that, honey. Actually, I wanted to tell you that school is closed until after the Christmas holidays."

Andi's eyes widened. "Why?"

"Dr. Weaver ordered a quarantine because of the number of scarlet fever cases."

Andi lost her appetite, even for sugary treats. She no longer felt sad because she couldn't be Mary in the pageant. Now, *none* of the townsfolk would enjoy the schoolchildren's retelling of the Christmas story.

"What about the pageant?" Andi sniffed back tears. "Our town's Christmas is ruined."

Justin took another cookie and smiled at Andi. "Oh, I wouldn't be so sure about our Christmas being ruined. I heard a rumor that the school's yearly Christmas pageant has not been canceled—merely interrupted."

Andi wrinkled her eyebrows. "Huh?"

"So long as no new cases of scarlet fever break out, Miss Hall hopes to present the pageant on New Year's Eve. By then, you'll be well enough to take up your role as Mary and—"

"Really?" Andi stifled a squeal. Mother would scold if she heard hollering from upstairs. She glanced around the room. "Where's my Bible? I need to relearn my lines!"

"My soul doth magnify the Lord, and my spirit hath rejoiced in God my Savior."

It was easy for Andi to put feeling into her words tonight. Her whole heart was praising God by the time she recited, "for He that is mighty hath done to me great things; and holy is His name."

He *had* done mighty things for her. Playing Mary for half the town of Fresno was proof of God's goodness.

There were no new cases of scarlet fever. The townsfolk packed themselves into the community hall.

The angels sang sweetly, only muffing their lines once. Johnny Wilson told the Wise Men to find the baby king and report back. Only one shepherd boy tripped when the ragged group bowed down before the sleeping infant in Mary's arms.

Andi didn't have to work very hard to look *blessed and serene* during the final manger scene. She felt utterly worn out from the evening's excitement. She clutched baby Richard and hoped she didn't fall over with him into the feedbox.

When she swayed, Cory wrapped his arm around her. The crowd murmured their approval of Joseph's care for Mary.

Andi prayed that the last song, "O Little Town of Bethlehem," would end soon.

A bleating from one of the lambs on loan from a local sheepherder rose above the singing. *Baa, baa!*

A second lamb joined its brother. A small calf bawled and stretched its neck against the rope that tied it to the backdrop. *Moooo!*

The scenery wobbled. Andi hugged the baby a little bit tighter. Would the background stay put?

The choir of angels and shepherds finished their song.

Reverend Harris offered up a short prayer and dismissed

the crowd. He clearly did not want to keep praying until the calf brought down the house.

The applause thundered, waking the baby. Richard howled his unhappiness. Mrs. Samuelson rescued her son, thanked Andi, and moved off.

There was food and drink and fellowship in the large hall, enough to bring in the New Year with a bang.

Very soon, a New Year's ball would be in full swing at the Fresno House, the big hotel down the street. Rumors flew that fireworks would light up the sky at midnight.

Andi slumped against a bale of hay and closed her eyes. *Not for me.* She dozed off.

Chad's hand shaking her shoulder woke Andi with a start. "You did good, little sister. A more blessed and serene Mary I've never seen." He chuckled. "And I know the reason why."

"So do I," Andi murmured drowsily.

Chad hauled her to her feet then swung her up in his arms. "You're done in. Let's find the rest of the family and head home."

Andi nodded. She was too tired to reply. But she was not too tired to smile to herself. It had been a close call, but her Christmas had not been canceled after all.

Merely interrupted.

4. Andi's Christmas Ball

Chapter One

December 1879
This story is set three months before *Long Ride Home*.

Humming her favorite Christmas carol, "Angels We Have Heard on High," eleven-year-old Andi Carter applied the finishing touches to Taffy's grooming. A final swipe across the Circle C brand on her rump, and the palomino shone as golden as a new day. "This will be our best week ever," she confided to her equine friend.

Taffy nickered and swished her tail.

"I thought you'd never ask." Andi giggled. "It's just you and me and Luisa next week. Plus the cowhands, but they don't really count."

Taffy's head bobbed up and down.

"Yep. The whole family's going to the Christmas ball at the governor's mansion in Sacramento. Except for me. I'm not thirteen yet." She let out a relieved sigh. "Thank goodness."

Andi threw her arms around Taffy's neck.

"Last year it wasn't much fun staying home," she told her mare, "on account of that dreadful wind and rainstorm. I was stuck in the house all four days. But it was still better than dressing up and going to a"—she made a face—"ball."

Andi let go of her palomino's neck and stepped back. She could scarcely contain her joy. The early December weather was everything Andi could have hoped for. Sunny skies and warm temperatures. Perfect riding weather.

"Luisa will let us ride wherever and whenever want," she told Taffy. "And no big brothers getting after me for not finishing my chores. Yippee!"

Andi tossed the brushes, hoof pick, and mane comb into the grooming box and put it away. "I'll be back later this morning, after everyone leaves for the train station."

Taffy stamped an impatient hoof.

"Don't worry, girl, I'll be back soon." Andi skipped out of the barn, scurried up the back porch steps, and burst into the kitchen. "*Buenos días,*" she greeted the Circle C housekeeper.

Luisa gave a quick reply and went back to work.

"Andrea," Mother called from the dining room.

"Coming, Mother." Andi swished her hands under the kitchen pump, dried them off, and joined her family for breakfast.

After Chad offered a quick prayer, Mother smiled at her daughter. "While you were out with Taffy, the Smith boy delivered an early-morning telegram."

Andi's eyes opened wide. It was only seven o'clock in the morning. The telegrapher must have been up mighty early to copy a telegraphed message and send it out to the ranch.

"Who's it from?" she asked.

"Justin," Mother replied.

Andi brightened. Her oldest and favorite brother had been in Sacramento for the past two weeks. He was often in the capital, or in San Francisco. Lawyer business kept him away from the ranch for weeks at a time.

She missed him. "He's coming home right after the ball for Christmas, isn't he?"

"Of course. And he'll stay through New Year's Day."

"That's great news." Andi smiled wider. "I've missed Justin so much. I can't wait 'til he comes home. Maybe he'll go up in the mountains with the boys to cut down the tree this—"

"You'll get a chance to see Justin sooner than you expected," Mother cut into Andi's chatter. "His telegram includes a special request from Governor Irwin."

A tickle of uncertainty skittered up Andi's neck. See Justin early? A special request from the governor of California? As much as she wanted to see her brother, this did not sound good. There must be a catch hiding behind the telegram's words. She swallowed. "What are you saying, Mother?"

"You're going to Sacramento with us," Melinda told her. "Isn't that perfectly *thrilling*? You're lucky, Andi. I wasn't allowed to attend the Christmas ball until I turned thirteen. But Governor Irwin has asked for you, especially, to come along this year."

Andi's heart dropped like a stone to her stomach. She had never met the governor. How did he even *know* her? What was Justin up to?

"I'll help you find the perfect ball gown," Melinda gushed, "and then we'll—"

"Why does the governor of California want *me* at his fancy Christmas ball?" Andi interrupted. She could think of a dozen different places she'd rather go.

Mother picked up the telegram and read it aloud. Each word made Andi slump lower in her chair.

CIRCLE C RANCH
FRESNO, CALIF.
GOVERNOR IRWIN REQUESTS ANDI ATTEND THE BALL TO PARTNER WITH HIS SON WILLIAM. SORRY FOR THE SHORT NOTICE. WILL EXPLAIN EVERYTHING WHEN YOU ARRIVE.
JUSTIN

Andi's heartbeat pounded in her ears. "How could Justin do this to me? I have to dance with some strange *young man*?" She looked at Melinda. "You are much more suited to dance with the governor's son, big sister."

She turned back to her mother. "Please send a wire to Justin right away. You can send it when you go to town to catch the train. Tell him I can't possibly—"

"That will do," Mother said. "William is not a young man. He's a boy your age. Governor Irwin probably wants someone to keep his son company at the ball."

"How would *you* like to be the only kid at this fancy shindig?" Mitch put in with a grin.

Andi wouldn't like it. "I'd stay out in the barn with Taffy and let the adults dance to their hearts' content. Can't this William kid go out to his father's stables, or find a friend to spend the evening with?"

Mother brushed a napkin across her lips. "I'm afraid the governor doesn't have the luxury of letting his son hide away. Public office puts the entire family in the spotlight, so William is most likely expected to attend."

"But Mother," Andi tried again, "I'm not thirteen. Please

let me stay home. Taffy and I have it all planned. We're going to ride . . ." Her words trailed away at Mother's look.

"It's an honor to receive a special request from the governor, Andrea. Justin sounds delighted that you've been invited. Do you want to disappoint him?"

She could see her brother now, smiling proudly and solving the governor's "problem" by offering his little sister without even asking her. Dressing up? Dancing with a strange boy so he didn't feel alone at the ball?

What did William do last year? Or the year before that?

Mother repeated her question. "You don't want to disappoint Justin, do you, Andrea?"

Andi stared at her plate of quickly cooling eggs and ham. No, she didn't want to disappoint Justin.

But mostly she didn't want to disappoint Mother. She looked just as excited as Melinda to learn that her youngest daughter had been invited to the governor's Christmas ball.

All right then. Andi sucked in a breath, straightened up in her seat, and let the words Mother wanted to hear come out. "All right, Mother. I'll go to the ball and make the best of it."

Just like that, Andi's four-day holiday with Taffy went *poof*.

Chapter Two

Five hours later, the train chugged into Sacramento. Andi pressed her nose against the window and scanned the platform for Justin.

Where was he? Big brother had a heap of explaining to do.

The Carter family had almost missed their train. It took time to pack Andi's clothes. She'd watched Luisa, Mother, and Melinda scurry around. Meanwhile, Chad kept calling up the staircase, "We're going to miss our train!"

Mitch and Chad had hustled Andi and Melinda into the surrey and helped Mother up. Andi was tired before the long ride in the railroad cars ever began.

A cheery wave broke into Andi's gloomy thoughts. She let the window slam down into its wide crack and hollered through the large opening. "Hello, Justin!"

"Must you *always* shout like Chad?" Melinda scolded from next to her sister.

Andi didn't reply. She left the red-velvet seat and slipped between passengers leaving the car. "Excuse me, please."

A minute later she jumped off the metal steps and ran smack into Justin's arms. "I've missed you so much!" It was too late to go back to Taffy and the ranch, so Andi didn't give him a piece of her very annoyed mind.

At least not right away.

Justin hugged her and they waited for the rest of the family to disembark. Once the luggage was loaded in the coach, Justin gave the driver directions to the governor's mansion.

"We've been invited to stay with Governor Irwin," he told them. "I'm glad my telegram arrived in time to include Andi."

"What is all this kerfuffle about the governor's son?" Mother asked. "We whisked Andrea out of ranch clothes and into traveling attire as fast as we could, but we almost missed our train."

"William's cousin Sofia usually partners with the boy at the Christmas ball," Justin explained. "However, Sofia came down with a nasty cold and cough yesterday. On a whim, I offered to bring my youngest sister to keep William company. The governor was ecstatic and made it official."

He turned to Andi and smiled. "It's not every day you get a personal invitation to attend the Christmas ball at the governor's mansion."

"The ball is the talk of the town," Chad put in. "Biggest folderol in these parts."

Andi said nothing. Right now, she and Taffy should have been sailing over the rangeland, but instead she would shortly be sailing over a ballroom floor.

She shuddered.

Justin chuckled. "I appreciate your sacrifice, honey. I can only imagine how difficult it was to pry you away from Taffy." He winked, which told Andi he really did appreciate it.

Andi gave Justin a weak smile, forgiving him.

By the time the rented carriage pulled to a stop in front of the governor's mansion, dusk had fallen. The windows glowed golden in the setting sun, and Andi caught her breath. This place was fancier than Aunt Rebecca's mansion in San Francisco. *Of course, it is*, she scolded herself.

After all, their host was the governor of California. His house was probably the fanciest place in all of Sacramento.

There was no time to collect her thoughts. No time to take a breath and steady herself. The Carter family walked up the dozen-plus wide steps to the front door and rang the bell.

The door opened at once, as if the butler had been awaiting their arrival. "Good evening, Mr. Carter," he said in a deep British voice.

"Good evening, Devlin," Justin replied.

Everything happened even faster after the men exchanged greetings. Servants snatched up the luggage. Maids showed the family to their own wing of the mansion. It even had its own water closet.

Andi stepped into her room. A maid was laying out something deep blue and frilly across the big bed. When she saw Andi, she turned and smiled.

"It was such short notice that Mrs. Irwin took the liberty of borrowing one of Sofia's party dresses for you, miss." She stroked the folds. "Tomorrow I'll press the pleats and ready it for the ball. If it doesn't fit, the seamstress will alter it."

Andi nodded, speechless with surprise. Mrs. Irwin employed a seamstress? Melinda would love that!

Melinda and Mother had decided on their dresses several weeks ago. The boxes of folds and fluff had been carefully packed. No doubt the dresses were being hung up this very minute in their rooms.

"Dinner will be served at six-thirty, miss. The bell will ring." Without another word, the maid curtsied and left the room.

Andi was alone, but not for long. She gave the blue dress a quick brush of her fingertips then headed out the door to look for Mother and Melinda.

A blond boy a little taller than Andi blocked her way.

He looked her up and down. "So, you're the girl Father insists I partner with at the ball." He snorted. "You're nothing like Sofia."

Andi's eyebrows drew together. "That's because I'm *not* Sofia. I'm Andrea Carter. Who are you?"

"William Geoffrey Irwin the Third." He smirked. "Most definitely *not* at your service."

Andi bristled. Visions of the school bully, Johnny Wilson, flashed through her mind. "Then if you don't mind, please step aside. I'd like to find my mother and sister."

William moved out of the way, but he didn't leave Andi alone. Instead, he followed her down the hall.

"You might as well know, Andrea Carter, that I despise the annual Christmas ball. But Father insists I attend. I'm his son, and I must make an appearance." He rolled his eyes. "And horror of horrors if I should attend by myself. My cousin Sofia always accompanies me."

He sighed. "When she fell ill yesterday, I'd hoped Father would let me off. I could have amused myself up in my room, far away from the festivities."

Andi stopped short and whirled on the boy. "Well, William Geoffrey Irwin the Third, *you* might as well know that right now I could be grooming my horse for a swell ride in the morning. Instead, I was whooshed off the ranch without a by-your-leave, and with no one asking if I wanted to go. I was then stuck on a train a good part of the day. I only like coming to Sacramento during the summer, when I can go to the state fair."

William's eyes widened. "You mean you don't want to be here?" He grinned. "You don't like balls, either?"

Andi shook her head.

"I'm only here because my brother told your father that he had a sister near your own age. So then, your father gave my brother a special invitation to bring me along." She shrugged. "I came because I didn't want to disappoint Justin."

"I see . . ." William's voice trailed away. He looked at Andi with new interest. "I thought I'd be stuck with a prissy, giggly girl who'd give me sheep's eyes and go on and on about how honored she is to be invited to the Governor's Ball." He rolled his eyes. "I'd have to listen to her silly chatter day and night."

His smirk returned. "Do you know how to dance?"

"Yes, I do. My mother made sure of that, but valley kids mostly like barn dances. They're heaps of fun."

William laughed. "There won't be any barn dancing at the Christmas ball. Just waltzes and quadrilles and such-like."

Andi grinned. She liked his laugh. He laughed just like Cory Blake, one of Andi's best friends. "I know the waltz and the quadrille. My brothers take me around the floor when we attend the New Year's ball in Fresno." She raised an eyebrow. "Can *you* dance, William Geoffrey Irwin the Third?"

"When I must. Sofia says I'm the best dancer for my age in Sacramento."

"I'd rather be known as the best horseback rider for my age in Fresno County," Andi shot back.

William laughed again. "I don't think the next few days will be as bad as I imagined." He nodded. "Call me Will."

As much as Andi wanted to head back to the ranch as soon as she could, she found herself thinking the same thing as William. Maybe this week would be all right, especially when her mind's eye no longer saw bully-boy Johnny but a friend like Cory.

"You can call me Andi," she offered.

William leaned closer and whispered in Andi's ear. "After supper, come with me upstairs to my classroom. I want to show you something."

Chapter Three

All during the evening meal, Andi wondered what William Geoffrey Irwin the Third wanted to show her. He seemed like a nice boy, but memories of Johnny Wilson tumbled around in the back of her mind. Johnny sometimes acted nice on the outside, but then—quick as a wink—he turned into a horrid bully.

She had almost decided she'd better not take the chance, when Will plucked her sleeve and whispered, "Come on. Let's go."

The grown-ups didn't seem to notice or care, so Andi excused herself from the long, fancy dinner table and scurried after the governor's son.

William sprinted toward the staircase. "Come on!"

Andi ran up behind him. She stopped short on the first landing. A pure white cat with long, fluffy hair and a sour expression on its flat face hissed at her.

Andi looked closer. The cat's eyes were two different colors—yellow and green. *What in the world?*

Just then, the cat arched her back. Her tail turned into a bottlebrush. She swiped a paw at Andi.

Andi jumped back and caught the banister railing to keep from falling down the staircase.

She had never encountered such a strange cat. Her friend Brody's cat, Cleopatra (a spoiled indoor cat in San Francisco), had looked just like one of the Circle C barn cats.

And Cleo never, *ever* hissed at Andi.

"Stop it, Precious," William swiped his arm toward the cat. The cat flattened her ears against her head and growled.

Precious? Smothering a giggle, Andi dodged the cat and followed William higher and higher up the staircase.

"Precious is Mother's Persian cat," he said. "A downright unpleasant creature. She is spoiled rotten and simply despises strangers." He chuckled. "The cat. Not my mother."

For sure, the cat despised Andi. She shot a quick glance behind her shoulder. Precious had found her bed, a bright-red jumble of bows and ribbons. She glared at Andi, showed a mouthful of sharp, white teeth, then stuck her nose in the air and promptly ignored her.

Thank goodness!

William burst through a door halfway down a long hallway. Gas lights showed Andi the richness of the governor's residence. Carpet, rich wood walls, and paintings with gold-gilded frames lined the walls.

She stepped inside William's spacious schoolroom. A globe stood in the corner. Andi wanted to hurry over and spin it, but she didn't dare. All this for one student?

How lonely he must be!

Before she asked William if he had any classmates, the boy lifted the door to a large, wooden cage made of narrow bamboo strips.

Curious, Andi joined him. William must want to show her an exotic pet bird. Or maybe a bunny. Or even a large spider. Tarantulas made swell pets, but so far Mother had put her foot down on Andi having one for her own.

"Meet Nebuchadnezzar and Belshazzar," William said. "I call them Neb and Bel."

Two large rats squirmed in William's hands. One was gray. The other was white.

Andi jumped back. Spiders and snakes were one thing. Andi was used to them. Field mice made good hunting for the barn cats. They were almost cute.

But a *rat*? Worse. *Two* rats? Who would want such disgusting creatures for pets? They looked like valley gophers with tails. Long, bare tails.

And valley gophers were disgusting.

Shivers raced down Andi's spine. Then she realized that William was watching her carefully. His brown eyes sparkled, as if he were playing the greatest joke in the world on her.

Andi sucked in a deep breath. *Don't run. Don't shriek. Don't cry.* "I suppose you scare your cousin Sofia with these pets?" she said in a tight voice. "Well, you can't scare *me*."

Not much, anyway, she added silently. Her heart was thrumming twice as fast as normal.

"Cousin Sofia hates Neb and Bel," William said in a disgusted voice. "So does the household staff. Mother says I must keep my rats in the schoolroom, or she'll make me get rid of them." He looked at Andi and grinned. "I was kind of hoping you wouldn't be scared."

Andi bit her lip. The gleam in William's eyes had not been the look of a boy playing a mean joke on a girl. It was a look of hopeful excitement. He really did love his pet rats.

Andi's heart slowed. She watched William sit down and let Neb and Bel explore his lap. Their whiskers twitched. When he set them on the floor, they took off to explore under the table.

"Rats make good pets," he told Andi. "They're *very* clean. I bathe them once a week. They like warm water."

Andi didn't say anything. The more she studied them, the less they looked like valley gophers and the more they looked like overgrown field mice.

Maybe these white and gray rats were not as disgusting as she had first thought. "Could I"—Andi took a deep breath and let it out—"hold one?"

William nodded eagerly. "Neb's the friendliest. He won't bite or nip you. I promise." He took off after the white rat and returned, beaming. "Pet him and let him smell you. It tickles." He plopped Neb into Andi's lap. "He loves to be stroked and scratched behind his ears."

William was right. The rat explored Andi's lap, pushing his whiskery nose into the folds of her skirt. She giggled, scratched behind Neb's ears, and then looked up into her host's shining eyes. "He *is* friendly."

"Rats are smart too," the boy said proudly. "I've taught them all sorts of tricks."

Andi looked at the busy rodent with new eyes. "What kinds of tricks?"

William needed no encouragement to show off his pets' intelligence. Andi's eyes grew wide watching Neb and Bel shake paws with William. They stood on their back feet when William said "up."

The best trick of all was when Neb and Bel jumped through a small hoop.

Andi clapped and squealed. Never in her life had she seen such tricks! "Wait 'til Cory hears about this," she exclaimed. "He'll get himself a couple of rats faster than you can say 'Belshazzar.'"

"Who's Cory?" William asked.

"My friend. Cory lives in town, but he comes out to the ranch whenever he can. We love to race and fish together."

It was William's turn to look impressed. "You can jump on a horse and go wherever you want, whenever you want?"

"I sure can, at least most of the time. I have a golden palomino, and we ride all over my family's ranch, which is thousands and thousands of acres."

William sighed. "I have a horse. Ebony's stabled out back, but I can only ride him if Phillip, our groom, goes along. Sometimes I find the man quite tedious. Perhaps our family can visit your ranch and you can take me riding and racing."

Andi grinned. "I'd like that, Will. We would have a swell time."

Chapter Four

Andi and Will played with the pet rats the rest of the evening. The hours flew by. Andi lost track of the time.

Eventually, a maid stepped into the doorway of the schoolroom and jammed her hands on her hips. "Mister William, the missus's been lookin' for you the past hour. You have a busy day tomorrow, and it's way past time for retiring. Now, get along with you."

Andi glanced up at the schoolroom clock. It read a quarter to ten. Very late! She shot to her feet. "I'm sure my mother is looking for me too. I'd better go."

"Indeed, Miss Carter." The maid nodded. "Come along with me. I'll show you to your family's rooms."

"See you tomorrow," Andi shot over her shoulder.

"Maybe not." William returned Neb and Bel to their cage. "The ball's tomorrow evening, and I have to help the staff bring in evergreen boughs all afternoon. Plus, the tree needs some final touches."

"Maybe I can help," Andi offered.

"Father and Mother would be shocked if a guest helped decorate." He shook his head. "I'm afraid you'll have to entertain yourself for most of the day."

Andi's face fell. Just when she'd decided Will might be an interesting companion to pass the time until this awful governor's ball was over, he'd be busy. *What will I do all day?*

The next afternoon, Andi was still wondering how she'd pass the long, boring hours until the gala began. She'd chatted briefly with Will at breakfast, but then the butler, Devlin, whisked the boy away to climb a ladder or hand up decorations, or something that sounded exciting.

Justin left on business to "tie up some loose ends" uptown. Chad and Mitch found something to keep them busy, as well. Mother left to call on old and dear friends, leaving Andi and Melinda on their own.

Melinda contented herself with walking around the extensive gardens and sitting under the orange and lemon trees on this beautiful December day.

Andi found her sister leafing through a new issue of *The Youth's Companion*. "Hi, Melinda." She sat down beside her.

"Hello yourself." Melinda set the magazine aside. "Did Cecily manage to get that blue gown altered for you?"

Andi let out a long, tired sigh. "It took most of the morning. Back and forth. On and off. Over and over. I'm pretty sure Will's cousin Sofia will never fit into it again." She giggled. "Cecily had to take the seams in a couple of times. The dress is hopelessly altered."

"Mrs. Irwin will probably insist that you keep the dress," Melinda said, smiling. Dimples appeared in each cheek.

"Oh, yes. She told me Sofia will not want the gown back. Altering it to her original measurements will show the seams Cecily used for me." She shrugged. "Lucky me. It's not the sort of dress one wears to a barn dance."

Melinda laughed. "That's for sure."

Andi swung her feet, kicking at the pebbles under the bench. "Say, big sister, would you like to see something?"

"What?" Melinda asked. "Not spiders, I hope."

"Nothing like that." Andi laughed. "But they are animals. Will's most unusual pets. I bet you've never seen anything like them."

Melinda's eyes showed her curiosity. "Promise me it's not a tarantula or a snake."

Andi swiped her fingers across her chest and gave her sister an impish grin. "Cross my heart. They're furry and smart. Trust me, you won't be scared or even disgusted."

"All right then," Melinda agreed. "Anything's better than sitting here and reading yet another magazine. I mean, honestly"—she sighed—"it's too bad we can't help out with the decorating. 'Many hands make light work,'" she quoted a favorite saying from the ranch.

"Come on," Andi urged. "I'm sure William won't mind."

She grabbed Melinda's hand and led her inside the house and up the wide staircase. When Andi passed the second landing, Melinda paused.

"On which floor is this spectacle?" she asked, clearly concerned about taking liberties in this mansion.

As if to underscore her caution, Precious slipped out from behind a thick, velvet curtain.

Hissss. Then she flattened her ears and growled.

"What in the world?" Melinda stepped out of the way.

"Never mind." Andi waved her hand, dismissing the animal. "Precious is a spoiled Persian cat. William says she doesn't like anybody."

Melinda gave the cat another cautious glance and followed Andi up to the third floor. When Andi turned the knob into William's schoolroom, Melinda stopped her. "You ought not to walk into rooms with closed doors. It's not polite."

"William and I are friends. He won't mind. Honest."

She hurried through the doorway and led Melinda to the pet rats' cage. "Look. Aren't they adorable?"

Melinda shuddered. "Not really."

"Watch, big sister. You'll change your mind." Like a girl who had handled rats all her life, Andi showed off her new skills. It took no time to convince Melinda that these furry creatures were smart as tacks and friendlier than barn cats.

"I have to admit," Melinda said when Andi was putting Will's pets back in their cage, "these pets are not as disgusting as I thought they'd be at first glance."

Andi beamed. "I knew you'd—"

"Oh, no!" Melinda gasped. "Look at the time. We'll have to fly to get ready for the ball. Mother and the boys are no doubt home by now. We mustn't be late!"

Melinda was right about that. Andi secured the cage with Will's special stick and hurried to catch up with her sister. Without a backward glance, she dashed through the doorway and down the hall.

Chapter Five

"Oh, my goodness!" Andi felt her eyes widen.

A magnificent ballroom opened before her, bright and shiny. More than a hundred elegantly dressed ladies and gentlemen milled around. Young ladies Melinda's age wore light colors in tulle and gauze. A few were dressed in silk.

Like Andi, they all wore silk slippers. Unlike Andi, the younger and older women wore long white gloves that reached to their elbows. Andi's gloves reached just past her wrists.

In one corner, a small orchestra was tuning the instruments for the waltzes and quadrilles that would soon begin. Maids in crisp black uniforms with white aprons made their way back and forth, laying trays full of rich foods on long tables.

The focus of the ballroom was the Christmas tree. It rose at least twenty feet high and still did not touch the ceiling. The branches held candles, intricately cut-glass ornaments, silk bows, and shiny tinsel. The long strands of tinsel flickered, reflecting the candle flames.

The tree looked like it was raining silver. Andi had never seen anything like it before in her life.

William came up beside her. "What do you think?"

She turned to her new friend. "It's lovely!"

Like the rest of the gentlemen in attendance, Will wore a tight-fitting dress jacket and matching pants. A white vest with gold buttons peeped out from under the coat. A white collar with a tie encircled his neck. Leather boots and white gloves finished his outfit.

Andi stared. "You sure look different from the boys at McMurry's barn dance last fall."

"You do too," Will said. "You look better in that gown than Sofia ever did." He bowed. "I would be honored to partner with you this evening, Miss Carter."

Andi's cheeks burst into heat. When she looked up, Mitch was grinning at her. "Mr. Irwin," he said, addressing Will, "you must allow me to dance with my sister at least once tonight."

"Stop it, Mitch." Andi suddenly wished she was home riding Taffy.

"You look awfully pretty tonight, Sis," Mitch told her. "That blue gown and those ribbons in your dark hair match your eyes exactly. Cecily did a fine job making you ready for your very first ball."

"It will be my last ball if you don't stop teasing me," Andi hissed under her breath.

Mitch's eyebrows rose. "I wasn't teasing you."

"I'll make sure she saves one dance for you, Mr. Carter," Will said graciously.

"I'll hold you to that," Mitch said over his shoulder as he slipped past the youngsters. He disappeared into the crush of the ballroom crowd.

"Well?" William asked. "Shall we join a quadrille set? I hear the music starting up. It's the 'Blue Danube.'"

Thank goodness, Andi thought in relief. She knew that waltz backward and forward. She curtsied and let William lead her onto the crowded dance floor.

Overhead, much taller than they, gentlemen and ladies formed their quadrilles. Will seemed to take in stride the idea that he and Andi were the only children at the ball. It was clear he was used to all this folderal, and he sure knew his way around the dance floor.

Andi was determined not to miss one step. Not for anything would she trip, or twirl right when she should turn left.

An hour later, Andi admitted—but only to herself—that she was enjoying the ball. William chatted happily the entire time he took her around the floor. "I climbed the ladder and put the angel on the tree," he boasted.

Andi's gaze went straight to the top of the twenty-foot-tall evergreen. She gulped. "A ladder is too wobbly. I would climb the tree to get that high."

"Not me!" Will laughed. "You are much more fun than Cousin Sofia." He leaned close. "I'm not sorry she came down with her nasty cold."

Andi was still sorry she was not home with Taffy, but she didn't say it out loud. Will was nice, and it would be impolite to wish herself home. She smiled. "Do you think we could get something to eat and dri—"

A high-pitched shriek rose above the orchestra. Soon, a dozen women were screaming. They ran helter-skelter, trying to get away from . . . something.

Andi looked at Will. "What's going on?"

Will shook his head. He grabbed Andi's hand and pulled her through the dozens and dozens of dancers.

By now, many of the ladies were headed toward the doors. Will pushed against the tide of swishing, swirling skirts.

"Oh, Will! Look!" Andi gasped and pointed to the tree.

It trembled as if a giant's hand was shaking its branches. The glass ornaments clinked. A candle shook loose, sailed to the ground, and snuffed out.

Will's face paled.

"What is it?" Andi asked. "What's wrong?

Will ignored her and broke into a run. Andi stayed close to his heels. The two reached the Christmas tree just as a silky puff of white dashed under the branches.

"Precious!" Will hollered. "Oh, no!"

Andi gaped at the cat. Growling deep in her throat, Precious struggled up between the thick branches of the white fir. The tree trembled. The tinsel swayed.

"What's got into that cat?"

Andi spun around. Governor Irwin's face twisted into an infuriated expression. Hands on his hips, he watched the richly decorated, most beautiful tree in Sacramento sway and shake as if a gust of wind was blowing against it.

Another candle shook loose and toppled over. This one did not drop to the floor and go out. It sputtered then glowed brighter as the flame licked at the needles. A puff of smoke rose from the smoldering candle.

Three glass ornaments fell next. They crashed to the ballroom floor in quiet tinkles and a thousand pieces.

Andi's hands flew to her cheeks. She stood frozen in place, her mouth agape at this unfolding calamity.

The next instant, the answer to what had turned the Persian cat into a whirling disaster revealed itself. A large, gray "something" with a long tail launched itself from an outermost branch and sailed across the four-foot space to the heavily laden banquet tables.

Splat!

Will's rat Bel landed in a china serving bowl of raspberry cream pudding.

Shrieks erupted from the ladies who had stayed behind. The gentlemen guests gasped. No one moved. Mrs. Irwin covered her eyes and leaned against her husband.

A white rat leaped from the tree and landed on the top of a three-tiered lemon cheesecake garnished with candied orange peel and almonds. *Plop!* Down went the dessert when the rat scurried to make his escape. Faster than eye could follow, the white rat dashed under the table and vanished, with the gray rat close behind.

Seeing his rats safe from Precious, at least for the moment, stirred Will into life. "Help me catch them, Andi!" Without waiting for a response, he dove under the tables and scrambled after his terrified pets.

Andi dropped to her hands and knees, lifted the snow-white tablecloths, and crawled in after Will. The tables seemed to extend for yards and yards. "Will!"

"Hurry!" Will shouted. "I see them." A pause. "Neb, Bel. C'mere. That's a fellow. It's all right. I'm here." He lurched forward.

The rat let out a long, drawn-out squeal then was silent. "Here's Neb." Will shuffled around and held out the white rat. "He's scared. Rats hardly ever make any noise people can hear. Comfort him if you can."

Andi took Neb and held the trembling pet close.

Will went after the other one.

Me—ow!

A dreadful yowling burst from the top of the tree. Neb firmly in hand, Andi crawled out from under the table and rose to her feet. "Oh, my."

Precious hung onto the top of the tree, meowing for all she was worth. She clearly had no idea how to get down. The angel swayed back and forth with the Persian cat's every yowl.

Andi couldn't help it. Clutching Neb against her chest, she started laughing. Precious looked anything but precious hanging from the tree for dear life. Why didn't she let go and crawl down the branches?

Will popped out from under the table holding Bel. He came and stood next to Andi. Instead of laughing, he shot a quick glance at his mother and father then jabbed Andi in the side. "Shh," he warned. "This is not funny."

Andi looked around the ballroom. Her family stood watching the display. They were not laughing. Neither was the governor, nor his wife. Mrs. Irwin looked close to tears. Andi wasn't sure if it was because the ball was ruined, or because she was upset about her stuck cat.

The governor's household was clearly not amused. The guests looked appalled. Andi's laughter died in her throat. The governor shouted orders for the ladder to be brought in.

Will's eyes widened. "If they think I'm climbing the ladder to rescue Precious, they have another think coming," he whispered to Andi. "I don't care for heights. I nearly fell off the ladder slipping the angel on."

Andi didn't smile. Will looked scared.

When the ladder was set up, Will shook his head.

His father sighed.

Precious yowled louder. She wouldn't stop. The entire ballroom was silent except for the cat's desperate meowing.

The tall, wooden stepladder fell short of the tree's top. No wonder Will was afraid. He must have stood on the very top of the ladder to add the angel topper.

There was no chance he could balance up there and nab a scratching, yowling cat. Then Andi got an idea. It was not her best idea ever, but it might work.

Maybe.

Chapter Six

"Here, take Neb." Andi pressed the white rat into Will's arms. "I'll climb the tree and get the cat."

Will's eyes nearly popped out of his head. "Are you crazy? It's twenty feet up there and"—he swallowed—"that cat will scratch you to ribbons."

"We'll see." Andi took a deep breath and headed for the Christmas tree.

She was an expert climber of eucalyptus and oak trees. She didn't get much practice climbing fir or pine. Those were mountain evergreens. But how hard could it be? So long as there were branches to hang on to, there was no tree Andi could not climb.

"Here goes nothing." She ducked close to the trunk.

"Andrea!"

Mother's voice turned Andi's head. "Yes, Mother?"

"This is not a good idea."

Chad grinned. "Andi doesn't weigh much. She's the only

person here besides Will who can do this, and the boy has his hands full." He chuckled. "Literally."

"Chad and I will hold the tree still," Mitch said.

Two other guests offered to help.

By the time the men steadied the huge tree, Andi was halfway up. As she climbed, she blew out the candles.

She didn't want to be caught in a tree on fire.

Fifteen feet off the ground, Andi poked her head out through the branches and grinned down at her family.

"I'm fine, Mother," she called.

Mother looked fearful. "Be careful."

"Andi climbs trees like a monkey," Melinda assured their mother. "Don't worry."

Mother wasn't worried about her daughter merely climbing a tree. Andi knew it was what waited at the top that might cause a problem.

When Andi emerged near the highest branches, Precious's meowing changed to low growls. She hissed at Andi and swiped a clawed paw at her.

"Stop it," Andi ordered. She reached out a tentative hand. "I'm trying to help you."

Another low growl told Andi that Precious did not want her help. Her ears lay flat against her head.

Andi pulled back her hand and paused. She had rescued her friend Brody's cat once, long ago. Cleo had run away after an earthquake and hidden herself under the shelves of Aunt Rebecca's deserted stables in San Francisco. Andi had caught Cleo by being quick.

She shimmied herself up until she was nearly eye-level with Precious. The tree began swaying.

"Ohhh!" She clutched the treetop.

"Steady," a voice urged the others at the base.

"Andrea!" Mother said. "Come down this instant."

"Yes, indeed," Mrs. Irwin said. "A cat is not worth injury, my child. Come down."

"All right!" Andi called. "I will."

Quick as a wink, she reached her hand above the cat's head, grabbed the scruff of her neck, and lifted her from her perch. Thankfully, the cat wasn't too heavy. She was all fluff. Andi held her easily.

Precious turned into a screaming, hissing ball of fur. Her legs flailed. One paw swiped Andi's forearm, leaving a bloody streak. She winced. *Ow!*

Finally, when the cat figured out that she couldn't get away from this wretched human girl, she went limp.

"That's better," Andi said. "Hang on. We'll get you out of this tree." Then she lowered her voice. "Serves you right, though, for chasing Will's rats all over the place."

Precious glared at her and growled.

Andi wasn't quite sure how she would climb down the tree holding a cat in one hand. Her grip was already loosening.

"Drop the cat, Andi," Justin called up to her.

"What?" She looked down.

Justin, the governor, and two other men held the ends of a large, white tablecloth. "We'll catch the cat."

"It's the only way," Governor Irwin agreed.

It was true. It was the only way Andi would make it down the tree in one piece. Gripping the treetop with one hand, she extended her other hand as far away from the branches as she could. "Here she comes."

Andi let Precious drop.

Five seconds later, it was all over.

The cat landed in the tablecloth, and the men lowered her to the floor. Precious took off like a streak of white lightning.

Andi scurried down the tree and emerged to the applause of the large crowd. They cheered and smiled.

Mother hurried over and embraced her daughter. Then she held her out at arm's length. "Look at you! Fir needles everywhere. Your hair is a tangled disarray, and your white gloves are bloody." She shook her head. "The gown is probably ruined."

"But the cat's safe," Andi replied brightly.

"So are Neb and Bel," Will said, joining her. His arms were empty. "They're back in their cage."

"Young man," his mother said. "What did I tell you about those rodent pets of yours?" She sounded furious. "They are a disgrace, and somehow you let them out. You will have to get rid of them."

Will looked crushed. "I didn't let them out, Mother. I promise. When I took them to their cage, it looked like the cat had chewed her way through the bamboo slats."

"Goodness gracious!" Mrs. Irwin's hands flew up in the air. "Still, it's your responsibility to keep your pets secured at all times. How did Precious get close enough to chew through their cage? Did you leave the door to your schoolroom open?"

Will shook his head. "No, Mother. I check the door every time I go in and out. It was closed all day."

"Nevertheless, William, you must get rid of those rats as soon as possible. I will not allow another disaster like the one this evening to occur. You clearly have not been diligent enough to—"

"Oh, no!" Andi gasped at a sudden, horrid thought.

All eyes turned on her.

Her cheeks flamed. "This is *my* fault, Mrs. Irwin. I took Melinda into the schoolroom to show her Neb and Bel."

"That's right." Melinda nodded.

"I didn't think Will would mind," Andi continued. "I made sure the rats were secured in their cage before we left, but Melinda and I saw the time. We were late to head back to our rooms to get ready for the ball, so we rushed out of the room. I thought I closed the door, but I was in such a hurry that . . ."

Her voice trailed off. She looked at Will. "I'm sorry, Will."

Will shrugged and looked at the floor.

Andi turned back to Mrs. Irwin. "Please don't make Will get rid of Neb and Bel. It's not his fault the cat found her way into the schoolroom and chewed open their cage. I bet the rats were terrified. No wonder they ran down the stairs, into the ballroom, and up the tree. I'd run too if I saw Precious's huge mouth and those eyes staring at *me*, and those paws full of claws and—"

"That will do, Andrea," Mother said.

The governor's guests were smiling. A few chuckled. One older gentleman guffawed and slapped his knee in mirth.

Mrs. Irwin sighed. "All right, my dear. You have made a good case. I will give Will a second chance. After all, you did save Precious."

She turned to her guests. "The staff have already cleared away the damaged food and replaced it. They've cleaned up the mess. Let's not have this little misadventure ruin our Christmas ball."

"Absolutely not," Governor Irwin said. "Orchestra, play. Let's get on with the festivities."

Before Will could coax Andi into joining him for a quadrille, Mitch spirited his sister onto the dance floor.

"My turn." He smiled. "You beat all, Sis. You're a sight to behold, but this will be a Christmas ball nobody will ever forget."

Andi smiled back. Mitch was right about that!

5. Andi's Icy Christmas

Chapter One

December 1880
This story takes place a couple of weeks after the events in *Andrea Carter and the Family Secret.*

Andi Carter hunched over her school desk and wrote quickly, churning out seven lines of perfect script in her copy book. Every line except the last began with a date and ended with an event.

"*¿Qué haces?*" Rosa hissed in forbidden Spanish, leaning close to Andi's dark head. "That does not look like your spelling lesson."

Indeed, it was not the page of words Andi had spelled wrong during her recitation. She should be copying "sufficiently," "transcendent," and "truculence" five times each, in order to prepare for Friday's final spelling bee. After that, school would be let out for the Christmas and New Year's holidays.

Three weeks with no school. She could hardly wait!

Andi already missed Levi, Betsy, and Hannah. Their train had chugged away to San Francisco last Sunday, leaving Andi behind, bored and restless. *Just when Levi and I were getting along so well too*, she silently mourned.

It had taken Andi two full weeks to recover from her dunking in the swollen, raging creek, and then *bang!* Just like that, her nieces and nephew had been whisked away to their new lives with their mother, Katherine, and Aunt Rebecca.

Boy, oh boy, are they ever in for a surprise! Aunt Rebecca takes some getting used to. She muffled a giggle and poised her pen over the final line in her copy book.

"¿Qué haces?" Rosa repeated a little louder. She had already finished her own spelling words. Easy English words like "muffin," "halter," and "courage."

"I'm not doing anything important," Andi answered in a low whisper. She uncovered her hand from her copy page and allowed Rosa to peek at what she was up to.

December 1874. Sid brought Riley's mother to the Circle C. Aunt Rebecca gave me a scratchy red dress.

December 1875. Mitch made up a treasure hunt for Riley and me. It ended at the kitchen, where Luisa and Mother helped us pull taffy.

December 1876. Riley left the ranch. I gave him a photograph of him, me, Taffy, and his horse.

December 1877. The boys and I went up to find a Christmas tree. There was a big blizzard, and we spent the night snowed in under the wagon.

December 1878. I was Mary in the Christmas Pageant, which was almost canceled when I and a lot of other kids came down with scarlet fever.

December 1879. Our family attended Governor Irwin's Christmas Ball. I met William and we played with his rats. I climbed the ballroom Christmas tree to rescue Precious, their cat. I danced a little bit.

December 1880.

Rosa's dark eyebrows rose. "¿Qué es esto?"

Before answering, Andi glanced up to see what their schoolmaster was doing. It would not do to be caught in trouble, not with barely three days of school left. She let out a relieved breath to find Mr. Foster engrossed in a geometry lesson with two of the older boys, Seth Atkins and Johnny Wilson.

"This is my holiday list," she told Rosa. "I am attempting to record everything I can remember my family doing for the Christmas holiday over the years. Sadly, I can't recall much from the Christmases when Father was alive, except for one thing." She paused, a gentle smile curving her lips. "Each time he and the boys came back from the mountains with the perfect tree, he would toss me up in the air."

Rosa nodded respectfully, her eyes dark and thoughtful. "That sounds like a lovely memory to have of you and your *papá.*" She placed a slim, tanned finger on the December 1880 date. "This one is blank."

Andi nodded. "I'm thinking hard of something special for this year's holiday. I sure don't want to attend any Christmas balls, not *this* year. There's a new governor, Governor Perkins.

Did you know he has seven children?"

Rosa smiled. "Maybe some of them are your age and you would have a girlfriend to—"

"No, thanks," Andi said. "I asked Justin about Governor Perkins's family. He frowned at my question and shook his head. That is *not* a good sign. I think he knows more than he's willing to share, but the good news? So far, Mother has not said one word about attending any balls." She smiled. "Maybe the Carter family did not receive an invitation."

Rosa did not get a chance to respond. A noisy clearing of his throat warned Andi that Mr. Foster had heard chatter of which he did not approve. She quickly turned the page and began to tediously copy her spelling words five times each.

By the time the Carter family sat down to supper that evening, Andi had turned holiday ideas over so many holiday ideas in her mind that her head throbbed. *Another trip to cut down a Christmas tree?*

No. Since Kate and the kids had left, Andi wanted to think of something the rest of family might enjoy together, not just she and boys running off on another Christmas-tree jaunt.

Give in to Aunt Rebecca and gather for Christmas in San Francisco? She made a face. *Oh, please, not that!* Andi didn't think she could be that "good" and ladylike for three or four whole days. Even if she would see Levi and the girls.

She sighed and stabbed her fork into the warm piece of dried-apple pie Luisa had set before her while she was musing. She'd barely noticed when the housekeeper had carried away her half-eaten bowl of beef stew and replaced it with the pie.

What about—

"There's our old hunting lodge in the mountains up past Lone Pine," Chad said. He forked a bite of pie into his mouth, chewed, and swallowed. "No one's used the place in years."

Andi's ears pricked up in interest. She'd been so immersed in her own thoughts that she hadn't realized the whole family was making Christmas plans around the table. *Hunting lodge? Mountains? Snow?*

"That's because in the winter, it's such a long way from here," Mother reminded her son. "We can't simply go over the Sierra this time of year. And what about supplies? We would have to haul them in." She shook her head.

"Ah, Mother," Chad replied, grinning. "Where's your sense of adventure? The lodge is huge, with plenty of space for the entire family. Mitch and I could go ahead and get everything ready. Justin would accompany you ladies a few days later." He turned to his brothers. "Right?"

Justin nodded. "Sure, Chad. But give me enough warning so I can clear my office calendar through the New Year."

"I'll come along with you, big brother," Mitch said. "That snug, log lodge is perfect for a family holiday."

Andi had remained quiet as a snowflake during this exchange. Hunting lodge? *What* hunting lodge?

"What about you, Melinda?" Chad probed.

"Yes," Mitch put in. "Care to join us, Sis?"

Melinda cocked her head, wrinkled her forehead in thought, then answered, "Yes, I believe I would. I haven't seen the lodge since I was a little girl, when Father took us there for a long summer holiday to get away from the valley heat." She smiled. "I've never been there in the snow, but"—she paused—"how long would it take to get there?"

"Only two days," Justin answered thoughtfully. "These modern times have seen a railroad boom. If we take the train through Bakersfield to Mojave, there is a new, narrow-gauge railway that runs north to Lone Pine. From there, we can—"

"*What* hunting lodge?" Andi burst out.

She couldn't keep still for one minute longer. *What other things have I missed out on that everyone else, even Melinda, knows about*, she wanted to accuse, but prudence kept her words tucked behind her too-quick tongue. The best way to learn something was to listen more and argue less.

Mother paused with a forkful of dried-apple pie halfway to her lips. "Your father and a prospecting friend built it years and years ago." Her expression turned soft and wistful, as if remembering special times. "We spent our bridal trip in that lodge. It was a wonderful two weeks exploring the high country. I learned to shoot and bagged a wild turkey, which we ate. Nothing tasted better than that bird, roasted to perfection over the fire."

"There's good fishing up on Cottonwood Lake," Justin remembered. "We could try ice fishing." Big brother was clearly warming up to the idea of a long Christmas getaway in the wilderness. "In fact, I remember when . . ."

Andi rolled her eyes. *Here we go again*. She sensed a story coming on, one that either included Andi as a baby or worse, a story where she hadn't even been born.

Good thing Katherine was not seated around the supper table tonight. She and the three older boys could go on and on reminiscing until—

"Shall we call it a plan then?" Chad broke into Justin's story and Andi's thoughts. He reached across the table and snagged her uneaten pie. "You don't want this, do you?"

He slid her slice onto his plate. "Don't look so glum, little sister. As soon as you see the lodge, everything will come back to you."

Andi doubted that.

A hunting hideaway during the summer would look quite different from a lodge covered in a foot or more of snow.

"Father took us all there, even you," Chad was saying. "It was the summer before he—" He broke off when Andi flinched. Chad scooted the plate toward her. "Listen, Andi, I'm sorry I brought Father up. Here's your pie."

Andi shook her head. "No, thanks. I'm not really hungry for apple pie right now, anyway. It's yours. Go 'head. Eat it." Relief that she hadn't missed *every* part of the Carter family's adventures settled over her like a comforting blanket. Maybe she would remember the lodge when she saw it. She hoped so.

A big, rambling hunting lodge made of logs, just like a mountain man's? The whole family—well, maybe not Kate and the kids, who were committed to sharing Christmas with Aunt Rebecca—together in a snug place Father had built years and years ago?

Andi watched Chad enjoy his second piece of pie—*her* pie—and a tickle of excitement swirled around in her belly. Father never did anything by halves. Wasn't the sprawling hacienda on the Circle C evidence of his extravagance? The Carter hunting lodge probably boasted a rough-hewn but magnificent staircase up to a second floor, with a landing that overlooked the downstairs.

Elk and deer heads decorated the walls. Glass windows with thick shutters kept the snow and cold out of the lodge.

Best of all, surely a fireplace made of mountain stones took up an entire wall and blazed with a cheery fire day and night.

Andi smiled. She could see it all in her mind's eye. Right after supper, she scurried upstairs to her room and flipped through her copybook to her page of notes.

December 1880. We will spend Christmas at Father's old hunting lodge in the Sierras.

Chapter Two

Andi wanted nothing more than to skip the rest of the school week and help with travel preparations. Mother said no, so Andi slouched in the rig to and from school and dreamed of snowmen, snow angels, ice fishing, and the biggest Christmas tree in the Sierras.

Rosa's eyes lit up when Andi shared her holiday plans with her friend. "¡Qué maravilloso!"

It does sound marvelous, Andi thought. *Too bad Rosa*—

"Justin!" Andi sat straight up in the buggy and clutched her brother's driving arm. "Could Rosa come along on our Christmas getaway? Please?"

Rosa ducked her head while Andi rattled on about sharing the holiday with her best friend. "Nila could come along too and help with the meals. After all"—Andi smacked her lips—"what's Christmas without *tamales*?"

Justin winked. "It does sound like a *maravilloso* plan, honey. I'm sure Mother would agree." He paused. "Unless Nila and Rosa do not wish to be separated from their own family over Christmas. We can't ask that."

"*Está bien, señor.*" Excitement tinged Rosa's words. "*Mamá* will be happy for me and grateful for the invitation. Joselito and *Papá* will not mind, either. We can celebrate our own *Navidad* or *Año Nuevo* when *Mamá* and I return."

Justin nodded. "Yes, we will certainly be home before New Year's."

Rosa sounded very sure of her mother's response, and it turned out exactly as she predicted. The Garduño family expressed their surprise and awe at the invitation. They could not do enough to help the family get ready.

"I will take special care of Taffy while you are away," Joselito promised. Not a twinge of envy colored his voice. He seemed genuinely pleased at his sister's and mother's good fortune.

"You shall have the best *tamales* north of the border for your *Navidad*," Nila promised, beaming.

Luisa pitched in to make sure Nila included everything she needed to keep her promise.

"We don't need to haul in *all* of our supplies," Chad announced that evening when the family gathered in the library. "Contrary to what I told you at supper the other evening, Mitch and I also don't have to go early to open up and restock the lodge."

Justin glanced up from the list he was composing at his desk. "Oh?" He paused his pen just above the inkwell. "Why not?"

Chad looked sheepish. "I remembered yesterday that Father had hired a caretaker in Lone Pine to oversee the lodge, keep a look out for squatters, and make sure there was always plenty of firewood and supplies on hand."

Justin put down his pen and leaned back in his chair.

"You're right. I forgot about that. Asking the caretaker to open the lodge and get the fire going will make our arrival much more pleasant. It will save a lot of time if he can check for supplies too."

"I'm one step ahead of you, brother." Chad pulled a telegram from his vest pocket and held it up. "I sent a quick wire to Mr. Lurry this morning, and here's his reply. He assures us the lodge will be ready for our arrival. If we wire him a list of supplies, he'll take care of restocking the kitchen."

"Very good," Mother said. "That means we can leave a day earlier than planned, since we needn't bring supplies."

Andi and Melinda glanced at each other. "Hurrah!" Andi shouted. She shot to her feet. "I'd best tell Rosa to start packing."

Rosa had never traveled aboard the railroad cars, and Andi determined that her friend would have the very best seat, a window seat. From there, she could watch the valley rush by faster than a galloping horse.

By the time the train carrying the Carter family, plus Nila and her daughter, arrived at the narrow-gauge railway station, Rosa's eyes were nearly popping from her head. She'd barely said more than a few sentences during the two-day trip. Mostly, she stared out the railroad car's window, her dark-brown eyes wide and alert.

"I feel like a *princesa*," she whispered as the engine carried the handful of passengers closer to Lone Pine.

"*Mira*, Andi." She pointed out the window. "*Soy una princesa de la nieve.*"

"We're *both* snow princesses," Andi told Rosa.

Never had the Sierra range looked so close. Just beyond the glass, Mt. Whitney's snowcapped crown towered over everything. It felt strange to be looking west to see the mighty peak. Andi had always looked east to gaze at the Sierras.

No wonder this trip had taken two whole days. They had been forced to go around the mountain range rather than over it.

"Snow is so cold that it burns your fingers," Andi said, watching a few flakes scurry past the window. "I remember from the trip I took with the boys one year." She shivered. "But the lodge will be warm and cheerful, I promise."

She'd also promised Rosa plenty of thick outerwear and woolen mittens. "We'll have snowball fights up where the snow is deep. When we tramp inside, shivering with cold, our mothers will make us steaming chocolate—"

A high, shrill whistle cut through Andi's snowy plans. She clapped her hands over her ears. "That's loud!"

The next instant, the train jerked and slowed. Another whistle. Huge clouds of steam puffed past the windows. The metal wheels braked and squealed, as if the mountain-climbing engine was catching its breath and its balance on the narrow track.

Andi leaned across Rosa and pushed her nose against the window. The steep incline fell behind, and the train chugged smoothly through a small valley and into the tiny town of Lone Pine, California.

Chapter Three

The train puffed, jerked, and squealed for a second time before braking to a stop. Andi should have been prepared. She wasn't. She flew forward, catching herself just in time before her nose hit the back of Melinda's seat.

"For pity's sake, Andi." Melinda peeked around the edge of her seat. "You should know better by now."

Andi didn't reply, although silently she admitted Melinda was right. She *should* know better, but her mind overflowed with so many exciting possibilities now that they were here in Lone Pine that she had forgotten. From under her seat, she yanked out a woolen coat, mittens, and a warm fur hat and put them on. Rosa watched with wide eyes then copied everything Andi did.

"Come on!" Andi grasped Rosa's hand.

"Stay close to the station, Andrea," Mother warned. "It will be dark soon."

"Yes, ma'am." Andi and Rosa left the train and stood on the snowy depot. To the west, the winter sun perched atop a tall peak. It wouldn't be long before it dropped behind the Sierras, but right now, the sun's feeble rays fell in bright splotches on the snowy main street.

"This town looks like one of those Swiss villages in my geography book," Andi said. "All white and sparkly."

Rosa clasped her arms around her middle. "*Tengo frio.*" Her teeth chattered.

"You'll get used to the cold," Andi assured her, as if she'd grown up with snow all her life. Which she hadn't. "You just have to make sure that you—"

A sudden icy *something* plopped against the back of Andi's neck. She whirled, brushing the snow from her hair and neck.

"Who did that?" she demanded.

Nobody confessed, but Chad's eyes twinkled. He looked too busy, however, to have lobbed at his sister's back. He was too far away too.

Just then, Melinda brushed up against her. "I heard you boasting to Rosa about getting used to the snow. I thought I'd remind you how cold snow really is, Miss Know-it-all."

Andi's mouth dropped open. Then she laughed. Her sister was right. Andi knew less than nothing about snow and cold. "I'll get you for that, you know, and when you least expect it."

"You can try." Melinda giggled and turned back to help Mother.

Rosa was still shivering, even in her fur-lined coat and hat. As much as Andi hated to admit it, she was getting cold too. A melted remnant of the snow blob dripped down her back, and she shivered.

"Why don't I accompany you ladies across the street, and we'll warm up inside the general store," Justin suggested. "Chad has to get in touch with Mr. Lurry, and Mitch is headed for the livery. He'll rent the sleighs as quickly as possible, and we can head up to the lodge. It's another hour into the mountains, so we don't want to linger. The sun goes down quickly in a mountain town."

"A sleigh?" Andi's words came out in an astonished whoosh. "With jingle bells and everything? Is it a one-horse open sleigh?"

Justin grinned. "Probably not. It will be an open sleigh, but more than one horse must pull this crew and all our trappings. Now, let's go warm up before we head out." He turned to Mother. "Unless you'd prefer we spend the night at the hotel and start for the lodge in the morning."

"I think we would all rather settle into the lodge tonight, even if it means riding in the cold for an hour," Mother replied.

"My sentiments exactly," Justin agreed.

A few minutes later, they crowded into the rough general store. A blast of heat hit Andi in the face, and she looked for the source. A red-hot potbelly stove glowed in the middle of the room.

Two older men sat nearby, balancing a checker board across their knees. They looked up, doffed their hats at the ladies, and went back to their game.

At the far end of the store, a counter of what looked like half a giant tree sawed down the middle stretched from wall to wall. Someone slung a load of furs down on the counter in front of the shopkeeper, and the two started haggling.

Andi stepped away from the stove. "One minute we're freezing, and the next minute we're roasting," she told Rosa in an undertone. "I can't imagine how that fur trapper can stay bundled up in here." She ripped away her hat and let her braids hang free.

A loud, cackling laugh from the trapper stirred Andi's curiosity. When she drew closer, the heavily wrapped person scooped up a gunny sack of supplies, left the furs behind, and headed for the door, looking neither to the left nor right. He scurried through the door and out into the waning light.

"He's in a mighty big hurry," Andi said.

"She's got a long ways to go," the shopkeeper said. "On foot, pulling a sled."

Andi's eyebrows shot up. A *lady* fur-trapper?

The shopkeeper took the lid from a jar of lemon drops and offered Rosa and Andi the candy. "That's old Maddie," he explained when Andi and Rosa each took a piece. Andi took an extra one for Melinda.

"She's a fur trapper?" Andi asked, popping the sweet into her mouth.

The shopkeeper nodded. "Maddie's a strange old coot but harmless enough. Lives up in the woods in a little cabin, perfectly content to while away the hours with the birds, bunnies, and other forest critters. Traps them too."

He held up a sleek, shiny fox fur. "She brings me only the best. Trades her furs for supplies."

Andi stroked it. "It's beautiful."

Melinda wandered over just then. She accepted the lemon drop from Andi and listened to the shopkeeper's description of Maddie.

"Poor creature. Lost her family in that earthquake back in '72," he said, shaking his head. "Worst quake in California history."

Melinda nodded. "We felt the tremors on our ranch near Fresno. I was pretty scared."

Andi wrinkled her brow and did the arithmetic. She'd only been four years old in 1872 and didn't remember any earthquakes. She'd felt her first earthquake a few years ago when she stayed with Aunt Rebecca in the city.

That one was scary enough!

Andi peered past the fur-wrapped customers in the crowded store to see where Maddie was going. "Will she truly walk through all that snow this evening? What if it gets too dark?"

"Don't worry about old Maddie, miss," the shopkeeper soothed. "She's got a lantern and can take care of herself. Why, just last year she—"

"Andi! Melinda!" Justin's voice cut through the confusion of the crowded room. "Mitch has the sleigh. Let's go before night falls completely."

"It was nice talking with you," Melinda told the shopkeeper politely. She, Andi, and Rosa weaved their way through the furry bodies and across the shop, where the door stood wide open.

Chad appeared. He shook a tall, bearded man's hand before waving at his sisters to hurry. *That must be Mr. Lurry*, Andi decided.

Andi drew her warm hat onto her head and stepped out into the darkening evening. Two large sleighs rested just beyond the porch. *Our sleighs!*

She held back a squeal with difficulty. Two bright lanterns

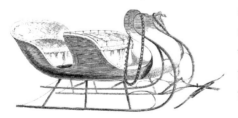

sat affixed to the front of each of the sleighs. There would be plenty of light to see along the snowy trail.

"Don't stand there gawking, Andi," Chad ordered. "Climb in. It's not getting any warmer."

Andi jerked her attention to the lead sleigh. Melinda, Mother, and Justin were already squeezed in front. Nila had settled into the back seat, so Andi took Rosa's hand and scrambled into the back of the sleigh with Nila.

There was a pile of thick fur robes underneath which Andi and Rosa buried themselves, giggling. "Look." Andi pointed to the east. "There's the moon. We get a moonlit sleighride." She shivered in delight . . . and with a little cold.

A silvery sound tinkled in the air when the horses shook their manes. Andi grinned. "Sleigh bells and everything!"

Justin spoke to the horses, and they were off, the runners sliding effortlessly over the snow.

Right behind Andi and Rosa, Mitch and Chad drove the second sleigh. The family's baggage and personal supplies were piled high in the second seat.

"Are you cold?" Andi asked Rosa half an hour later. The moon played hide and go seek with the tall, dark evergreen trees that lined the path. Right now, the moon was hiding. Only the lanterns' dim glow lit the trail.

Mr. Lurry had clearly worked hard to clear a path to the Carter hunting lodge. Andi snuggled deeper into the warm sleigh robes and waited for Rosa's reply.

"No," Rosa said quietly, "I am quite warm." She lay back against the seat back and turned her face to Andi. Her dark eyes glowed. "*Oh, gracias, mi amiga. Soy muy feliz.*"

"I'm happy too," Andi agreed. "I think this will turn out to be my favorite holiday outing of them all."

She looked up and watched the dark silhouettes of the forest trees rush past. The stars twinkled in the navy-blue sky. As much as she tried to keep her eyes open, the warm buffalo robes, swishing sleigh runners, and jingling bells lulled Andi into a drowsy contentment.

Before she knew it, the sleigh was pulling up to a drifted snowbank. Chad yanked off the fur robes and shook Andi awake. "C'mon, sleepyhead. Let's go!"

Brr! She wasted no time clambering out of the sleigh and along the narrow path between the snowdrifts. A yellow glow shone from two of the windows, but the rest of the building lay shrouded in shadows too dark to make anything out.

Right now, Andi didn't care what their family's grand hunting lodge looked like. She was too sleepy. In a daze, she climbed the porch steps, stumbled through the great oak door, and headed for the wide staircase to the second floor.

"Don't you want supper?" Justin asked.

Andi yawned and shook her head.

Mother shushed Justin and followed Andi and Rosa up the stairs. "I'll show you girls your room," she offered.

A few minutes later, Andi felt herself drifting off to sleep next to Rosa, in a big feather bed covered with warm quilts. She didn't remember washing up, saying her prayers, or even bidding Mother and Rosa good night.

Chapter Four

The next two days slid by in happy abandon. The hunting lodge was everything Andi had hoped for and more. The fireplace's wide, gaping mouth held large armfuls of split pine and fir, which kept their home away from home warm and cozy.

Mother enjoyed reading or knitting in front of the fire, while Melinda waffled between romping outdoors with Andi and Rosa and relaxing on the rug to let the heat soak into her bones after a wild snowball fight.

On the morning of the third day, Andi and Rosa leaned over the wide railing on the second floor landing and watched the boys struggle with the fifteen-foot red fir they had cut down the afternoon before. The girls had stayed behind and helped Mother and Nila roll out cookie dough and cut out bells and stars and trees.

"I bet that tree falls *smack* in the middle of the great room before the boys can get it up," Andi told Rosa. "I hope Melinda and Mother stay out of the way." She grinned, hoping to see something interesting. Christmas trees rarely cooperated on the first try, especially tall ones.

"Your brothers do all things well," Rosa replied. "I think the tree will go up on their first try, with no mishaps."

"If I were a gambling girl, I'd make a wager with you," Andi challenged. "But I'd better not."

Rosa giggled. "We shall see who is right, though."

Andi rolled her eyes when less than an hour later, the tree stood exactly where Mother had directed, and on the first try. The branches dripped with leftover bits of melting snow that clung to the needles, even after a good shaking before coming indoors.

It was a beauty! A silvertip fir tree, perfectly symmetrical. The cones stood upright on many of the branches and looked like little brown candles.

"You're right, Rosa," Andi admitted cheerfully, "and I'm glad." She picked up a cutout cookie and munched on the sugary confection. Crumbs spilled down her chin. "We would have spent the rest of the morning picking up loose needles had the tree come tumbling down."

It would be another day or two before the tree dried out enough for the decorations, but the whole lodge soon filled with the fragrance of a pine forest. "It smells like Christmas," Andi said, taking a deep breath.

The sun stood as high as it ever did in December, and the snow sparkled like a thousand diamonds. After luncheon, Andi and Rosa pulled on their outerwear for a romp in the snow.

"Melinda," Andi called. "Are you coming with us?"

Melinda strolled to the back door and shook her head.

"No, thank you," she said. "I'm still licking my wounds from yesterday's defeat. Maybe later this afternoon, I can convince Mitch or Chad to join our snowball fight. Then I will have a fighting chance against you two."

Andi laughed. "All right. Tell Mother we'll be exploring new paths in the snow."

"Don't wander too far," Melinda warned. "You don't want to get lost in the woods."

"We can't get lost," Andi scoffed. "Rosa and I have explored most of the woods nearby. Even if we don't see the lodge or the smoke from the chimney, our boots make huge prints and a fine trail. The clearing around the lodge is all trampled down. Rosa and I want to find fresh snow, the kind that makes the best snow angels."

"I suppose you're right," Melinda said. "Have a good time."

Andi shut the door behind Rosa and herself and stepped off the porch. The air was icy but clean and crisp.

Rosa had adjusted to the mountain weather and no longer complained of being cold. *How could she be*, Andi wondered, *bundled up in a fur coat with flannel petticoats under her skirt, two pairs of woolen socks, mittens, and a warm scarf and hat?*

By the time Andi led Rosa deeper into the forest, her breath came in gasps. The early afternoon sun might not be warm enough to melt the snow, but Andi was melting from the inside out. Tramping through knee-deep or higher snow was no easy task. Sometimes, a wrong step plunged her and Rosa up to their hips in an extra-deep drift.

Andi yanked Rosa up from another misstep and fell laughing backward into the white fluff. She took advantage of her position and moved her arms back and forth, creating a lovely snow angel.

Never had she had so much fun! Snow was certainly God's gift to children. Andi could not get enough of it, even when her fingers and toes tingled from the cold.

Rosa peeked behind her shoulder. "I hope we have not come too far." A worried tone filled her voice.

"Even if we have, look." Andi pointed to the path their feet had made. "Nobody could miss that trail. We'll find our way back. *No te preocupes*." Then she stood still. "Listen. Do you hear that?"

In the snowy silence, Andi recognized the sound of running water. Justin had mentioned a lake and ice fishing. Where there was a lake, one often found a stream.

"Water?" Rosa wrinkled her eyebrows. "Would it not be frozen solid in this cold?"

"I don't know." Andi shrugged. "Let's go see."

It didn't take long before Andi and Rosa stood on the snowy bank of a wide creek. A layer of ice covered most of it, but here and there, running water kept the deeper parts of the stream ice-free.

"*Qué bonito*," Rosa admired.

The partly frozen creek *was* pretty. Evergreen branches hung over the banks, catching most of the snow, so it wasn't quite as deep here. This made for easier walking.

"Look!" Andi squatted next to a set of animal tracks. "I bet this one's a rabbit." She'd seen her share of rabbit tracks in the dust back on the ranch, and their prints looked the same in the snow. "Let's follow the tracks. It will be an adventure."

"What about these?" Rosa asked, taking the lead.

Andi stood up and joined her friend. "They look like coyote tracks. Maybe it's a fox, like that trapper lady brought to the general store."

Andi and Rosa made a game of finding tracks and trying to identify the animals that had made the prints.

"Deer, maybe," Andi decided a few minutes later when she discovered a new set of tracks. These looked like the prints the Circle C cattle made in the dirt but were much smaller.

Farther down the creek bank, Andi couldn't begin to guess the owners of these other tracks. Beaver maybe, or raccoons? "This is fun!"

Rosa sighed. "Too bad we cannot scoop up the snow and take the tracks back to the lodge."

Andi stopped short. "I have a better idea. Tomorrow, we'll come back. I'll bring paper and pencil and we can draw the tracks. Then we'll see if the boys and Melinda can guess the animals that made them."

"*Qué gran idea*," Rosa agreed. Then her dark eyes turned worried. "Do you suppose we will find bear tracks?"

Andi laughed. "Bears hibernate."

"Hi-ber-nate? What is this word?"

"It means the bears curl up in their dens all winter and rarely come out. So, I don't think we'll come across any bear tracks, thank goodness."

The girls continued downstream, but the animal tracks became more difficult to make out. Andi kept walking but looked up to check the time. "The sun goes down early this time of year, especially in the mountains. We'd better go back before somebody comes looking for us. We'll be in big trouble if they—"

Snap! Clang!

Pain as sharp as a knife gripped Andi's left ankle and did not let go. She gasped and collapsed to the ground in agony, stifling a scream.

Had a bobcat attacked while she wasn't paying attention? Maybe a badger. Or worse—a wolf? Gritting her teeth against the pain, Andi looked around for the source of her throbbing injury.

She caught her breath. No animal had attacked her. Her ankle was clamped in the vicelike grip of a small, steel-jawed animal trap.

Chapter Five

Tears burned Andi's eyes and spilled down her cheeks. She couldn't stand. She couldn't move. When she tried to shift her foot, a sharp pain shot up her leg.

"Rosa!" she cried. "I'm stuck. *Really* stuck."

Rosa fell to Andi's side. Her white face showed her fright. "Stand up, *mi amiga*. I will help you. We have to go home." She grabbed Andi's arm and yanked.

Andi shrieked. "I can't. It hurts too much." She reached out and tugged on the trap's long chain. It was well staked and didn't budge. "Even if I could stand up, how far could I walk dragging this thing behind me, even if you could pull the chain free from the ground?"

"I will pry open the trap. You must help me. We have to free your ankle." Rosa started crying. "We must *try*."

Gritting her teeth, Andi nodded. Rosa was right. "Maybe my ankle won't hurt as much if we free it."

Andi knew her thick, fur-lined leather boots had saved her ankle from the horror of broken or crushed bones. However, the stabbing pain told her that the trap had pierced her skin and torn into her muscles. She had to get free!

Her friend's idea might be her only hope.

Rosa took hold of sides of the trap and pushed down on the springs.

Andi gripped the trap's jaws with shaking hands. She held her breath and strained against the tightly closed teeth. "It's working," she gasped. The pain eased when the trap began to open.

Suddenly, Rosa lost her grip. The springs slipped from her hands, and the metal teeth snapped together. Andi screamed.

"*Lo siento, lo siento*," Rosa sobbed her apology. "My fingers slipped. The springs are too strong, and my mittens are too slippery."

"I k-know," Andi stammered. "We can't pry it open far enough to slip my boot through. We're not strong enough."

Andi sat back, clenched her jaw, and relaxed her leg. The pain lessened a tiny fraction, so long as she kept her foot still. Or maybe it was growing numb. *I can't think about that.*

Rosa's sobs rose, tearing into Andi's thoughts. Her friend was mumbling, praying in Spanish so low that Andi could not make out what she was saying.

Andi prayed too, prayed for wisdom. It was growing darker. It must be late afternoon. Worse, they had wandered far along the creek bank, where the snow was not deep enough to leave a good trail.

They could not stay out here much longer. "You have to backtrack to the lodge," she decided.

There was no response.

"Rosa!"

Her Mexican friend looked up with red-rimmed eyes.

"You have to go back to the lodge and bring help," Andi told her. "My brothers are strong enough to open this trap."

She forced a teary smile. "I'll stay right here. I promise."

Rosa did not laugh at Andi's attempt to lighten the mood. "I will not leave you," she insisted.

"Then we will freeze to death before anybody figures out how far we've come. They will follow the trail but then what? Did we go upstream or downstream? Even a lantern won't show our path along the creek bank very well, not in this shallow snow."

Rosa appeared to be pondering.

Then the worst happened. A few snowflakes began to fall. No wonder dusk was settling in faster than usual. Clouds had gathered. Andi hadn't even noticed, not with the tree branches hanging over the bank.

The branches might keep most of the snow off, but out in the open, where they had trampled down a trail, the snow would fall faster. Soon, their path would be covered.

Andi's heart plunged to her belly. "Rosa, you have to go *now*, before snow covers your path home. Before it gets too dark to see the trail, and too dark to bring help. Please, Rosa, go *now*."

Rosa nodded and rose to her feet. "*Sí, mi amiga. Yo sé.* I know." She laid a mittened hand on Andi's head. "May God protect you."

"And you," Andi whispered.

Rosa turned and scurried back upstream. Soon, she was swallowed up in the shadows, and Andi was alone.

"Oh, please, God," Andi prayed. "Bring my brothers soon."

If for some reason they could not pry open the steel jaws, one of the boys would pick her up and carry her back to the lodge, trap and all. "But I'm sure they can open the trap."

Her mind warmed up to the vision. Chad viciously tearing the steel jaws apart in less than a minute; Mitch gently guiding her injured foot from the trap's deadly grip; Justin snuggling Andi in his arms for the trip back to the lodge.

Andi blinked. The comforting vision vanished. Snow continued to fall. It blanketed the animal tracks just beyond where she sat, numb with pain, under the spreading evergreen branches.

Andi shivered. Sitting still, the chill of a snowy, late afternoon settled into her bones, except for her injured ankle. It throbbed, giving off a feeling of searing heat. She pulled her hat farther down on her head, tightened her scarf, and wrapped her arms around her knees.

More tears welled up, but she blinked them back. *I will not cry. It won't bring help sooner. Instead, I will pray that Rosa does not lose her way. I will trust and not be afraid.*

After praying for Rosa's safety and for her brothers' speedy arrival, Andi began to count. She knew it took about a quarter of an hour to count to a thousand. Another thousand, and a whole half hour would pass, so long as she counted slowly and didn't rush. Counting would also keep her awake.

Time passed. The shadows deepened. "Two thousand five hundred twenty-five, two thousand five hundred twenty-six, two thousand five—"

Swish, swish. The sound of someone or some*thing* coming across the snow caught Andi off-guard. She lost her place counting and held her breath. Wolf? Bobcat? *Oh, please, God! I'm so scared, and I hurt so bad. Help!*

A high-pitched, cackling laugh cut into Andi's desperate prayer. "He-he! Look what I caught in my trap."

The fur-wrapped figure drew closer. "You ain't a fox or a beaver, dearie, are ya?"

Andi's heart raced. She recognized the laugh. She'd heard the same laugh only a few days ago in Lone Pine.

Old Maddie, the lady trapper.

Chapter Six

Andi didn't answer Maddie's silly question. Of course, she was not a fox or a beaver.

It appeared that the trapper didn't expect an answer. Instead, she started talking.

At first, Andi thought the old woman was speaking to her. It didn't take long, however, to figure out that Maddie was talking to someone inside her own head.

This idea unsettled Andi and made her heart pound. She swallowed her fear and tried to ignore the agony spreading up her leg.

"Didn't I tell you it was a good idea to collect the traps before the snow covered them?" Maddie paused, as if listening for a reply, and chuckled. "Yes, dearie, I know. It was your idea. But it was me that heard the child counting. Her voice led me right to the poor thing."

Another pause. "Yes, of course we will take her in. It won't do to leave her out here, not with the weather building up to give us quite a pile of snow."

Maddie yanked on a rope, and a long wooden sled slid into view. A number of traps, along with a freshly caught fox and two beavers, lay atop the sled. As did a brightly lit lantern.

"Old Maddie won't let you freeze to death out here." She shuffled closer. "Let's see what damage Iron Jaws has done."

With surprising gentleness, the old woman patted Andi's head and got down to business. She was a small woman, but her gloved hands looked powerful. "There's a trick to convincing Iron Jaws to let go of his prey, but don't you worry, dearie. He always obeys his mistress." She cackled, sending chills up Andi's neck. "As soon as I open his mouth, move."

Andi shrank from Maddie and watched her step on the springs on each side of the trap. Then her strong hands spread the iron teeth apart. "Hurry," the old woman ordered, panting at the effort to hold the trap open. "Iron Jaws does not like keeping his mouth open for long."

Andi obeyed. She scooted backward, barely managing to keep from crying out as she dragged her injured ankle across the snow.

Clang! The trap snapped shut on empty air.

Laughing, Maddie pulled up the stake with one hand and tossed the trap onto the sled with the others. "Don't pout," she scolded. "You will get your iron jaws on another critter soon enough. When the snow stops, we'll set our trapline farther upstream, nearer the lake. We always have good luck there."

Andi had not said a word all this time. She huddled in pain, shock, and confusion. The Lone Pine storekeeper had told her Maddie was harmless, but he'd never said anything about her being touched in the head.

Perhaps she behaves normally when she goes to town, Andi thought.

Maddie reminded Andi of Loony Lou, the grisly old man who lived up in the mountains near her home. She and Cory had spent a night with Lou a couple of years ago after Cory fell and hit his head during a gold-panning adventure. Andi still remembered her bewilderment when Lou called the bear rugs in his cabin by name.

Maddie cleared a space between the fox and beaver pelts then shuffled back to Andi. Grasping the back collar of her fur coat, the lady trapper dragged her over the snow to the sled.

"Upsy daisy," she said, plopping Andi into place. "You don't mind riding with Iron Jaws and the rest, do you, dearie? They're good company on a dark, lonely night." She peered at Andi through small, black eyes.

"N-no, ma'am," Andi whispered. Actually, she minded very much but was too dazed and hurting to say anything.

"That's a good girl." Maddie grinned. "You're a polite child, what with your 'ma'am' and all. Just like our Rosie."

Andi did not ask who Rosie was. She was afraid of the answer. Could Rosie be the child Maddie had lost during that earthquake so many years before?

Pulling her furry garment tighter around her middle, Maddie made her way to the front of the sled. She picked up the sled's rope hand and a lantern. "Don't you worry none, dearie," she told Andi when the sled began to move. "We'll get you home in no time and then we'll see to your injury."

She paused. "I shall be quite displeased if Iron Jaws has taken a bite from your ankle that cannot be fixed." She glanced over her shoulder at the pile of jingling steel traps.

"Do you hear me, Iron Jaws? You should be ashamed of yourself for biting a girl. Why, she's the spitting image of our Rosie. It's like you bit Rosie. Shame on you!"

With that, she yanked harder on the rope and headed downstream. Andi gripped the edges with both hands.

Whether Maddie was just a little "off" or crazy as a loon, Andi didn't know, nor did she care. She was comforted knowing she would not have to spend the night outdoors, alone and hurt. Especially with snow falling in big, whirling, white flakes and evening settling over the mountain forest.

She feared this dark, icy-cold forest more than she feared the strange trapper lady, who acted more like Loony Lou by the minute—crazy but kind.

At least for now.

Andi's last thought before drifting into a pain-filled sleep was of Rosa. She hoped with all her heart that her friend had found her way home before the snow and a fast-approaching night covered the trail.

Andi woke up with a gasp. Her ankle screamed with pain. When her eyes focused, she found herself propped up in front of a fire. Her wraps had been removed, and her boot lay next to the fire, sliced to the sole. *Where am I? What happened?*

"There now," she heard a gentle voice sooth. "It ain't too bad. No, not bad at all."

The voice triggered Andi's memory. She was in Maddie's cabin, with the woman hovering nearby. Andi pushed herself upright on both elbows to see the damage done to her ankle. Her foot lay soaking in a pan of what felt like boiling water, although she knew it couldn't really be that hot.

The water had turned red with blood. *My blood.* Puncture wounds from the trap's teeth circled her leg just above her ankle.

Everything looked swollen and bruised. Nausea churned Andi's belly, and she bit her lip to keep from crying out. She tried to pull her foot from the pan, but Maddie held it down.

"Patience, dearie. The stinging and throbbing will go down if you just have patience. I've put my best herbs to work in that pan, and I would not want them to go to waste. You keep those wounds in the water, do you hear me?"

Andi nodded and scooted to a sitting position.

Maddie stuffed furs and rough blankets behind Andi for extra support. "There now. The herbs should be doing their work soon."

To Andi's surprise and intense relief, the throbbing began to recede. In fact, her entire ankle was turning numb.

She sighed her relief. For the first time in hours, the pain was going away. "Thank you," she whispered, truly grateful to this strange woman. Whatever she had put in the water was having its affect.

"Open wide, dearie," Maddie said, pushing a spoonful of dark liquid between Andi's lips. "This will put you to sleep. When you wake up, your ankle will be dressed. It will still hurt, but there is no permanent damage. No broken bones. In a day or two, you will be walking around good as new."

She gave her strange cackle. "Iron Jaws did not bite as hard as he could have. Your strong boot kicked back, I dare say." She laughed again. "The joke was on him."

Andi's eyes grew heavy. No doubt Maddie had dosed her with laudanum, the universal cure for whatever ailed a person. Sleep came, but disturbing dreams followed.

Rosa was lost, wandering in the dark forest, calling for Andi to find her. But Andi could not. Her ankle was caught in the trap. She yanked the stake from the ground and crawled through snowdrifts higher than herself trying to find Rosa.

Then Melinda joined Rosa, and both were lost. Snow swirled around them, hiding the girls. "Rosa! Melinda!" Andi croaked.

Mother appeared and called for her daughter. Andi tried to answer but no words came. Then Mother, Melinda, and Rosa fell through the ice into the frozen creek and vanished.

"Mother!" Andi woke up, sweating. Drops beaded her forehead. "Mother!"

A snowy dawn peeped through the two small windows in Maddie's cabin. Across the room, the lady trapper lay snoring on her narrow bed. Andi's call had not awakened the woman.

Andi sat up. Mother did not come to her call. Neither did Rosa nor Melinda. They were not lost in the snowy forest or drowned in an icy creek, after all. It was all just a bad dream.

"I want to go home." Andi looked at her ankle. It was wrapped in thick, clean cloths. Her eye caught the remains of her boot. Even if she could put weight on her injury, she was missing a boot. Her foot would freeze.

Worse, she didn't know the way back to the hunting lodge. She had no idea where she was. Maddie's cabin might be halfway up Mount Whitney.

No, it was Andi who was lost, not Mother, Melinda, or Rosa. She glanced at the window. It was still snowing. She wasn't going anywhere. *I hope Rosa's all right.*

Chapter Seven

Chad stomped through the back door of the lodge, his arms loaded with firewood. He shook the snow from the shoulders of his heavy coat and walked through the kitchen and into the great room.

"Mr. Lurry is worth his weight in gold," he remarked, dropping his load into a bin next to the fireplace. "There's close to six cords of wood cut and stacked. It's nice to not have to split wood on my vacation."

Mother smiled at her son. "I see it's starting to snow."

Chad pulled off his hat and shook it over the hearth.

"A few flakes here and there," he said, "but those clouds look pretty thick. We might even get enough snow to cover up the trampling you girls made of the clearing."

He shot a teasing grin at Melinda then looked around. His smile faded. "Where are Andi and Rosa?"

"They went outdoors a couple of hours ago," Melinda said. "I suspect they're in their room now, thinking up snowball fighting strategies." She paused. "Speaking of which, I was hoping that you or Mitch might join me so we can beat those two girls. They tromped me yesterday."

Chad barely heard his sister's request. His brow furrowed. "I didn't see the girls' outerwear in the back entry when I came inside. Nor did I see them playing in the yard."

At Chad's words, Justin and Mitch grew alert. Mother set aside her needlework and sat up straighter. "They know they must be indoors before dusk," she said in a worried voice.

"Yes," Justin agreed. "It's not dusk yet, but the snow clouds are making it darker than usual for this time of day."

Melinda abandoned her book and hurried up the wide staircase. She was back in less than a minute, hanging over the landing's balcony. "They are not in their room."

"Where can they be?" Mother's voice caught.

"Don't worry, Mother," Justin soothed her. "They never go far. We'll take a look outside. The four of us will round them up in a hurry." He looked at Melinda.

She nodded. "The girls can't be lost. They need only follow their path back to the lodge. We'll find them."

"When we *do* find them," Chad muttered, "they'll have a lot of explaining to do." He looked at the oversized chair he'd pulled up next to the hearth earlier and sighed. "There goes my peaceful before-supper rest in front of the fire."

Mother stood. "I'm coming with you. I can check the trails as well as any of you."

Justin pulled her aside. "Nila will wonder what the fuss is about if we all leave the lodge," he said softly. "I suggest you stay behind and not worry her unless there is cause."

Mother sighed. "That does seem like the wiser thing to do, but I do not like the thought of my daughter and her friend out there, cold, frightened, and lost." She returned to her seat and picked up her needlework, but her fingers trembled. She looked up. "Please find them, boys."

Chad nodded, the earnest look in his mother's blue eyes making him feel guilty for his earlier grumbling. " We will, Mother. I promise."

The four Carters donned their warm winter gear and headed outside. It was still light, but the snow was falling in earnest now, coming down in large, wet flakes.

"It's beautiful." Melinda tipped her head toward the sky. "So silent, soft, and peaceful—"

"And the kind of snow that covers forest paths mighty quick," Chad cut in. "Come on, let's move."

They spread out in different directions, calling the girls' names.

Chad started up the trampled path at a fast trot. This trail looked fresh. It veered northeast, toward Cottonwood Lake. *Maybe the girls wanted to check out the lake for ice fishing,* he thought.

The lake wasn't far, but what if they walked out onto the ice and—

The thought of his sister or her friend falling through the ice turned Chad's trot into a run. He brushed past branches heavy with snow, sailed over a log half-buried in the snow, and kept his eyes focused on the compacted path.

Stopping to catch his breath, Chad cupped his hands to his mouth and bellowed, "Andi! Rosa! Where are you?"

He paused, waiting for an answer. Andi would not play hide and seek when Chad used that tone. She would answer if she were anywhere within shouting distance.

Chad heard nothing. He continued along the path, calling out for the girls every minute or two.

A sudden, sinking feeling slammed into Chad's belly like an icy fist. The trail was filling up fast. Already, the girls' boot tracks had vanished. His only guidepost was the path the girls had cut through the deep snow.

Dusk was falling. Soon, it would be too dark to see the trail. *Oh, God, where are they?*

A faint shouting arrested Chad's movement. He strained his ears. Was Melinda calling from the opposite direction?

Suddenly, a small figure bundled in thick outerwear appeared far ahead on the path. She staggered toward him. "Help!"

Which girl was it?

Chad leaped forward, closing the distance between himself and Andi or—

Rosa looked up into Chad's face. Tears streamed down her cheeks. "Oh, *Señor* Chad. Hurry! *Por favor.*" Rosa's words poured out in terrified Spanish. Chad couldn't make out a word she said through her blubbering and hiccupping.

He grabbed Rosa's shoulders and gave her a little shake. "Slow down. Stop crying. Take a breath and tell me what's happened. Where's Andi?" His heart raced.

Rosa sucked in a breath and slowed her words. They came out in gasps. "An animal trap . . . the creek . . . left Andi behind. M-must find help. I got turned around twice and couldn't find the trail . . . so scared. If I had not heard you calling us"—she panted—"I might still be wandering."

She sagged, sobbing as if her heart might break.

Chad wasted no time. He scooped Rosa up and made a beeline back to the lodge. Once there, he paused long enough to pull out his pistol and let off a round before going inside. His family would recognize the signal and return.

Good thing too. Darkness was settling in fast.

"*Sí, señor,*" Rosa said, "I can take you to Andi, but—" She glanced out the window and shuddered. "*¡Qué escuro!*"

"Don't worry," Justin assured her. "We have lanterns and horses. The dark won't hinder us. Let's hurry, though, before the path is completely covered with snow."

Rosa nodded. She wiped her swollen, watery eyes, hugged her mother, and followed Justin and Chad outside. Mitch had saddled three horses. He boosted Rosa onto Chad's horse, and soon they were off.

Chad held his lantern high, leading the way. He knew Rosa was a little wary of his bossy, no-nonsense ways, so he kept his voice as soft as possible so as not to frighten the girl.

She looked terrified enough as it was.

The sun had set, but no lingering rays of red or orange colored the snow. No moon, either. In its place, lacy-white flakes fell in an unending curtain. Lounging next to the fireplace, Chad would have delighted in the outpouring of this winter wonderland.

However, riding horseback in the freezing temperature, straining his eyes to follow the path Rosa pointed out, and worrying over his sister was not enjoyable at all.

Chad nudged the horse when it faltered and clucked his tongue when his mount balked at the half-buried log. His own horse, Sky, would have trotted or even galloped at his master's light touch.

Not this high-strung mare. She was clearly letting this upstart young horse-renter know that she preferred her warm stable and alfalfa rather than this cold, dark ride through an unfamiliar forest.

Chad kept the upper hand and urged the mare forward.

With the path nearly covered with snow, they finally reached the creek bank. Rosa sobbed her relief and slumped backward against Chad's chest.

He squeezed her shoulder. "Well done, Rosa. Which way? Upstream toward the lake or downstream?"

Rosa's mittened hand pointed to the right. "This way. It is

not far. We made a game of guessing which animals made the tracks, so we did not travel quickly. Then"—a sob—"the trap caught Andi and . . . and . . ." Her voice faded to a whimper.

"Andi!" Chad hollered. He raised himself in the stirrups and held the lantern as high as he could reach. "Answer me!"

Justin and Mitch pulled up alongside Chad. "Well?"

"Over there," Rosa said breathlessly. "Under the branches of that evergreen tree. That is where the trap caught Andi."

"You're sure?" Justin asked, peering into the deep shadows.

"*Sí, señor*," Rosa answered. "I am certain. I remember how the branches nearly touched the ground."

The brothers pulled their mounts to a halt and dismounted. Rosa stayed in the saddle, shivering.

They tramped through the snow, brought the lanterns close to the ground, and looked for a sign that their sister had been where Rosa indicated.

"She's not here," Mitch said in utter dejection.

"We're going to track up and down this creek until we find her," Chad said. "Come on."

Leaving the horses tied to the trees, Chad promised Rosa they would be back soon. "Here." He handed her his lantern and smiled. "Be strong."

"*Gracias, Señor* Chad." Rosa clutched the lantern in both hands. "I will pray for my friend."

Chad nodded. Then he turned away and hurried to catch up with his brothers.

An hour later, night fell completely.

Except for the yellow glow of the lanterns, the creek bank and surrounding forest were pitch black. The snow had let up, but not enough to discover any evidence of what had happened to their sister.

"Do you suppose Rosa was confused?" Mitch asked. "Perhaps we should look downstream a little farther."

"We must return to the lodge before we all get lost."

Justin's weary words stung Chad to the core, but he nodded his agreement. "Perhaps Andi was able to free the stake holding the trap in place and found shelter. It's the only explanation for why she's not where Rosa left her."

"I pray that is the explanation," Justin said. "I just don't think there is anything else we can do tonight." He paused. "But tomorrow? That is another story."

Defeated and near despair, Justin, Chad, and Mitch made their way back to the horses.

What will we tell Mother, especially after I promised her that we would find Andi? Chad cringed.

It was going to be a long, sleepless night.

Chapter Eight

"Please, ma'am," Andi pleaded when Maddie stirred from her cot. "Would you take me back to the lodge?"

Maddie looked at Andi as if she had lost her mind. "Nay, dearie. Nobody goes to that hunting lodge in the deep, dark forest." She offered Andi a wooden bowl filled with mush and lowered her voice. "There's some that say the old place is haunted. Whoever owns it ain't been there for years and years and—"

"It's my family's hunting lodge," Andi interrupted. "It's no more haunted than—" She stopped. *Than this cabin,* Andi had intended to say, but her hasty words might not go over well. The last thing she wanted to do was annoy Maddie.

Maddie looked alarmed at Andi's statement. Then she cocked her head as if listening to an inner voice. She slapped her knee. "You're right. The girl did crack a good joke. Not haunted!" She laughed. "Her *family's* lodge!" She laughed harder. "Imagine, making up fanciful stories!"

Maddie turned off her cackling as if she were shutting down a leaky pump and shook her weather-worn finger at Andi. "We won't listen to any jokes about that lodge, do you hear me?"

"But—"

"We always stay clean away from that place. Only the good Lord knows what sort of squatters and riff-raff hole up there." She made her way to her stovetop and dished a bowl of cereal for herself, muttering the entire time.

When she turned back to Andi, her eyes snapped. "Jackson says you're a bit touched if you think you can make us believe you come from that place." She shook her head. "No, dearie, you must be a runaway from town. Yes, that's it. Though the good Lord knows it's a far piece for a bit of a girl like yourself to travel in this weather."

"I'm no runaway," Andi tried to explain. *Who is Jackson?* "Rosa and I were following animal tracks when that trap of yours caught me and—"

"Rosie?" Maddie's head jerked up. "Another Rosie, you say? Is she out there too? Did you run away together?"

"She's back at the lodge, getting help." *She'd better be. I can't keep going 'round and 'round with this crazy lady trapper.*

Maddie crossed the room and towered over Andi's still form. "I told you, dearie. No more fool's talk about that lodge. I mean it."

Andi ducked her head and whispered, "Yes, ma'am."

"Now, that's better." Maddie's tone changed faster than a spring shower to sunshine. She finished her mush and began cheerfully pulling on her outerwear. "The snow's finished its work. I need to take Iron Jaws, Steely Eyes and the rest and set my trapline this morning." She chuckled. "If our friends do their work, I'll oil them and hang them up in their special places as a reward."

She rattled a trap. "Hear that, Iron Jaws? Time for work."

Andi's stomach turned over. "What about me?"

Maddie paused putting on her thick, fur-lined mittens. "Don't worry, dearie. There's plenty of wood for the stove. There's more mush or some jerky to chew on. I'll be gone most of the morning."

"B-but," Andi stammered, "I want to go home."

Maddie squinted at Andi. "Runaways never want to go back. You're safer here, away from whatever ruffian or orphanage you ran off from."

"I'm *not* a runa—"

"*I* say you are." Maddie suddenly looked in full control of her reason. "You will stay here. I won't let nothing bad happen to you. I like you, and I'm plenty lonely since Rosie and Jackson ain't around any longer. And those folks in Lone Pine? They're a tricky bunch, and you're well rid of them."

She finished dressing, gathered up the clanging, rattling traps, and headed outdoors. "I'll set my traps and come right back. Don't be afraid. You're safe with me. I promise."

You're safe with me.

Maddie's words sent chills skittering up and down Andi's neck. How crazy was this lunatic? Once she got a notion stuck in her head, it didn't appear like any kind of common sense would move her.

Andi had been wrong. This trapper was *not* like Lou. Lou had not been truly "loony," just old and lonely. He would not have left Cory and her behind when they needed him most. Instead, he cheerfully showed them the way home and gave them gold nuggets too.

Andi stood up and made her way to the window.

She rubbed the condensation from the filthy panes and watched Maddie lumber away, pulling on her large sled.

When the lady trapper vanished between the forest trees, Andi limped back to Maddie's cot and sat down. Tears stung her eyes. *How will I ever get back?*

Maddie had been right about one thing. Once the wounds were cleaned and dressed in tight wrappings, Andi's ankle didn't hurt as much as she thought it would. She'd felt only a dull throbbing when she walked to the window and back.

Andi rested for a few minutes, then she stood up and walked back and forth across the cabin's one large room. The more she walked, the less stiff her damaged ankle felt. Once, when she stepped on a stick of kindling, pain shot through her leg and briefly made her stomach roil, but she didn't care. She winced and kept walking.

As the morning dragged on, Andi's painful limp faded to only an annoyance. "Maddie's a good healer," she said, stopping by the stove for some hot water. "I've gotta get out of here," she told the stove, "before I start talking to you like crazy old Maddie does."

Andi's gaze landed on the tattered remains of her boot. Maddie had cut the sides clear down to the sole in order to pull it over Andi's swollen ankle and leg, so now she was bootless.

Or was she? Andi plopped down next to her footwear and examined it closer. The sole was in place, and the sides had been sliced but were still attached to the sole.

What if . . . Andi's heart leaped. Could she bring the side pieces together and wrap everything in strips of cloth around her leg? Maybe the boot would stay in place.

Then again, maybe not.

How long could her slapped-together boot repair last tramping through deep snow? Since the storm, the drifts had piled up higher than her head. Rising, Andi crossed to the door, swung it open, and stepped outside. To the west, Mt. Whitney displayed its snowy crown.

The peak glowed pink in the remnants of a late-rising sun. The rest of the directions—east, south, and north—led to forests and more forests. The icy creek was nowhere in sight. Andi didn't have any idea which way to go to find the creek.

She shivered and hurried back inside.

Andi shut the door against the bitter cold, returned to the pile of blankets she called her bed, and prayed, "Please God, show me the way home."

Then she let her tears come.

Chapter Nine

Morning inched its way toward noon, but Maddie did not return. Andi scrounged a biscuit and a piece of beef jerky. She spent an hour looking for rags to tear into strips for her boot. She'd found her good boot, along with her hat, mittens, and woolen scarf.

Not that collecting her outerwear did much good. Andi still didn't know which way to go. She stoked the stove with pieces of pitch-pine. The fire snapped, spreading its warmth throughout the cabin.

She sighed. Where was Maddie, for pity's sake? The woman was long overdue.

Look outside, a stray thought swirled in her head.

Andi strolled to the window and rubbed the dirt away. Dressed in so much winter gear that she resembled a fuzzy black bear, Maddie would be hard to miss against the dazzling snow.

But Andi saw no movement in the white wilderness. Nothing but dark-green trees, glittering snow, and two long tracks, where the sled's runners had passed into the forest.

Andi propped her chin in her hands and stared out the window for a long time. Her gaze was drawn to the sled tracks, and she willed Maddie to return. Even a crazy lady trapper was better company than a metal stove and a pile of dead animal pelts. *Why, oh why—*

Andi gasped as a sudden, unbidden thought slammed into her mind. *The sled tracks!*

"I'm not lost. I can follow those sled tracks back to the creek." Her family was surely looking for her while there was still daylight. Why, they might be pacing up and down the creek right now, watching for signs of Andi's passing.

"They might even run into Maddie," she whispered with growing excitement. Then she frowned. "Not that the trapper will tell my brothers a thing, not if she's hoping to keep me with her."

Suddenly, time seemed to fly. It was early afternoon. The sun shone, but if Andi wanted to grab a chance to go home, she must take it now. Once Maddie set her traps, she might not check them again for a couple of days.

The thought of even one more night in this cabin made Andi shudder. "I must go *now*."

She hurried to her torn boot, gingerly slipping it on over the thick wrappings. "Oooh," she moaned. Her ankle did not like being confined inside the too-tight boot sole. It throbbed in time with her heartbeat.

Gritting her teeth, Andi took the strips she had torn earlier and wrapped each one around her leg, securing the tall side pieces that came halfway to her knees. The dressing showed between the wide cracks in her sloppily repaired boot.

No matter, so long as it kept the snow out until she reached the lodge.

The rest was easy. Andi pulled her arms through the coat sleeves, pulled her hat down over her forehead, and wrapped the scarf around her neck. She slipped on her mittens and left the cabin.

She did not look back but focused on the sled tracks. They were easy to follow in the deep, fresh snow, as were Maddie's boot tracks. Even when they weaved back and forth through the forest, around trees and drifts that covered old stumps and dead logs, Andi had no trouble keeping sight of the trail.

Her breath came in ragged gasps. The sled and Maddie's boots had trampled a partial path, but the snow was deep. Not for the first time, Andi wished for a pair of snowshoes to ease her walking.

When she felt as though she had been walking for hours, Andi glanced up. The afternoon sun had not traveled very far. In the distance, she heard the familiar sound of the creek.

Andi pushed on and soon found the stream. The ground along the bank was trodden with multiple horse tracks. Her heart leaped. Tracks showed everywhere in the new snow—up and down the creek in both directions, as far as she could see.

Why, all she had to do was follow the tracks backward to the hunting lodge. *Thank you, Lord!*

She hurried on, ignoring the wet, icy feeling in her injured foot, until she came to a spot she recognized well. The huge fir, with its snow-laden lower branches that nearly touched the ground.

This was where she and Rosa had been when the trap snapped shut. Andi nearly burst into tears of joy. It would not be long now. The prints would guide her home! She set off at a brisk pace, as fast as her injured ankle allowed.

Soon, she would see the trail that led away from the creek and back to the lodge. When the well-trodden path appeared, Andi said a quick prayer of thanks and turned away from the creek.

Just then, a faint voice rose above the sound of the gurgling stream. Andi stopped in her tracks. "Help. Help." The voice was weak but clear.

Rosa? Andi sucked in a frightened breath. Could her friend have gotten lost on her way to find help? Had she spent the night out here? No, it wasn't possible. Rosa would not be alive in that case. But who—

Maddie! It had to be. She must have somehow fallen into the creek while setting her trapline. Or worse—Andi cringed—maybe she got bit by her own trap.

Andi gave a longing look at the horse prints leading back toward the lodge. Then she turned aside and headed upstream.

The lady trapper's cries were growing weaker, almost a whisper. "Help."

Andi watched her step while she made her way along the creek bank. She had no desire to find another of Maddie's traps. She saw a glint of metal under a bush near the water and skirted her way around it.

When she pushed through a tangle of winter-dead brush, Andi nearly fell on top of Maddie. The trapper's mittened hands clutched the frozen, muddy creek bank, but the rest of her body lay partway in the water. She had clearly broken through the ice. Why didn't she simply stand up and climb out?

The reason came quickly when Maddie glanced up. One side of her head was bruised and bloody.

"Maddie!" Andi gasped. "What happened?"

The old woman didn't answer. She looked nearly frozen and close to exhaustion.

Andi didn't know how she could help, but she didn't have time to run back to the lodge. She needed to pull Maddie out of the creek before she froze to death. Luckily, the bank was not steep. She grabbed Maddie's arms and with a mighty heave, she yanked. The small woman slid effortlessly over the ice and snow and dropped at Andi's feet.

Andi whirled. Maddie's sled lay close by. "Can you climb on the sled?" she asked.

Maddie nodded. The grim look on her face told Andi that the woman was determined not to die out here in the cold. Half-dragging and half-lifting, Andi helped Maddie onto the sled. Once there, the woman collapsed.

"Maddie?" Andi shook her.

There was no response.

Andi limped to the front of the sled and picked up the rope. By now, her injured ankle screamed at the abuse Andi had piled on it. Clenching her jaw, she shoved the pain to a corner of her mind and slowly dragged the sled along the creek bank.

What seemed like a long time later, Andi turned toward the lodge. She followed the trampled path until her arms felt like lead. One step. Two steps. Sucking in her breath, she staggered a few more steps.

Then she heard a delightful, most-welcome sound, the neighing and snorting of horses. Someone was coming up the trail! Her family had resumed their search.

She knew they would never give up. "Mother! Justin! Chad! Mitch! Help!" Her voice echoed through the forest.

Then the best sound in the whole world answered, her brothers calling out her name. "Andi!"

Snow flew from the horses' hooves as Justin, Chad, and Mitch pounded down the trail. Moments later, Justin slid from his horse and pulled Andi into his arms, squeezing her so tightly that her breath caught.

Chad was next, then Mitch.

Andi peered up into her brothers' cold, red faces and saw tears in their eyes.

"We thought you had perished," Chad said. "But for Mother's sake and for our own, we decided we would spend every day out here looking for you or for your—" He stopped. An expression of anguish mixed with relief at knowing his sister was safe covered his face.

Andi knew what Chad couldn't say—her body, frozen in death. She hugged him. "Maddie saved me from the trap and tended my foot."

She turned and pointed to the sled, where the lady trapper lay unconscious. "She needs help. Somehow, she fell in the creek and hit her head. I don't know how bad off she is."

The boys asked no questions but quickly sprang into action. Chad mounted his horse and took Maddie from Justin's arms. He left at a brisk trot and headed for the lodge.

Andi climbed up in front of Justin, and he and Mitch followed Chad. Now that the worst was over, Andi's ankle throbbed. She looked down. Blood oozed from between the cracks in her boots. Her wounds had broken open.

No matter. Mother would see to everything. She wriggled back into Justin's chest and relaxed.

Yes, Mother would make both her and Maddie well.

Chapter Ten

For two days, Maddie was too sick to be aware of her surroundings. However, Mother's gentle touch and Nila's herbal concoctions brought the woman back from the point of death. She seemed surprised to wake up in the land of the living.

"Where am I?" she croaked when her eyes cracked open.

"With friends," Mother assured her.

It wasn't until later in the week that Maddie learned she'd been taken to the "haunted" hunting lodge. She and Andi exchanged knowing glances, and Maddie kept quiet.

So did Andi.

Except for a lingering cough and fever, Maddie was healing well. The swelling from the knock on her head went down. She seemed to thrive surrounded by Andi's family. She sat in an overstuffed chair near the fire, a warm blanket spread over her knees, and rarely moved. She seemed happiest when her rough, red, chapped fingers strung popcorn and cranberries for the tree.

Only once did something seem to worry her. "If it ain't too much of a bother, I'd be obliged if somebody looked out for my traps. I don't want no animal suffering cuz I couldn't check up on old Iron Jaws and Steely Eyes."

Chad opened his mouth to ask what in the world the old woman meant, but Andi cut in. "I'll go along with Chad or Mitch to make sure your metal friends are cared for, and that any fox or beaver is dealt with."

Maddie nodded her thanks.

Chad gave Andi a puzzled look but said no more.

Christmas Eve settled over the lodge in the form of falling snow. This time, Andi was safely inside the hunting lodge, surrounded by her family and friends. They had planned an evening sleigh ride into town for the Christmas Eve service, but Maddie's fever and deep cough worried Mother.

Justin decided for them. "We'll all stay home this evening. I'll read the Christmas story from Luke two, and we'll put the finishing touches on the tree. Then we can light the candles and enjoy Nila's tamales, hot chocolate, and sugar cookies."

Andi nearly burst with happiness at Justin's words. As nice as a Christmas Eve service might be, it was, after all, being held in an unfamiliar church in Lone Pine, rather than in Fresno. She would much rather stay here and show Maddie that the Carter hunting lodge was not haunted, but was filled with the love of God and family.

Andi had decided early on that she would make no mention of the crazy talk from a lonely old woman who had lost her family so many years ago. Instead, she would stick to her story that Maddie had been kind, rescued Andi from a frozen fate, and tended her wounds with care.

All of this was true. There was no need to add more, at least not today. Maybe Andi would tell Mother later.

When Justin hung Maddie's popcorn strings over the tree branches, and the last of the candles were carefully lit, the family gathered in front of the fireplace.

Andi and Rosa found places on the thick rug in front of the fire and lay back to listen to Justin read from Luke.

He opened the family Bible and began reading. "And it came to pass in those days, that there went out a decree from Caesar Augustus that all the world should be taxed."

Justin finished with, "And the shepherds returned, glorifying and praising God for all the things that they had heard and seen, as it was told unto them."

Andi sighed, perfectly at peace.

No one spoke. Justin closed the Book and set it aside.

In the silence, a faint whimpering came from Maddie's direction. She wiped her eyes with a corner of her lap robe and said, "I have been alone too long, and it's my own fault. I am grateful that the little girl fell into my lap, so to speak. I tended her, sure, but for selfish reasons, which I won't go into."

Andi let out the breath she was holding. *Good.* She didn't want her family to hold anything against this poor old woman. What if they learned Maddie had meant to keep her? And that she listened and talked to not only voices in her head but also to most everything else in her house? They'd think she was crazy.

Maybe she *was* a little crazy, Andi admitted to herself. But it was most likely a kind of crazy that came from shutting folks out and spending too much time alone.

Maddie took a deep breath, coughed long and hard, and went on. "I believe you folks have brought me back to my senses. Folks in Lone Pine have tried to befriend me, but I didn't trust them. Maybe it's time to let God take care of the past."

She sighed. "I haven't heard the Christmas story read like that for many a year. It's a time for new beginnings."

Maybe being around other folks would keep the voices from the past out of her head. Andi sure hoped so.

"When I'm up to it, I think I'll go into town and talk to Joe, the shopkeeper, about helping him around the store. He's asked me plenty of times. Says it ain't healthy to be alone so much." She coughed. "I s'pose he's right."

Before anyone could respond, Nila's proud and happy voice called out from the dining room. "*Señores, señoras, y señoritas, por favor*. The best *tamales* north of the border are now ready to be served. They are best served hot."

Chad and Mitch raced to the dining room. Justin offered Mother his arm.

Andi leaped up. "Hurrah!" She pulled Rosa up beside her. "What did I tell everybody? It's not Christmas without your mama's *tamales*."

Rosa giggled her agreement.

Maddie's voice rose above the clamor. "Hey, now. What is she jabbering about in that foreign tongue?"

Andi eyes opened wide. "Have you never eaten a *tamale*, ma'am?"

"No. I don't go in for those foreign foods."

Andi and Rosa looked at each other in surprise. "They are a Mexican dish always served during the Christmas holidays," Andi explained. "You'll like them."

Maddie looked skeptical. "If you say so."

Andi hurried to the kitchen and filled a plate with the steaming, cornhusk-wrapped delicacies. Nobody in all of California—or Mexico, for that matter—made tastier *tamales* than Nila.

While the rest of her family piled their plates high with *tamales* and other dishes, Andi slipped back into the great room. She served Maddie the plate of *tamales*, along with a cup of hot Mexican coffee, and sat down beside her.

Maddie looked around. Finding the room empty, she whispered, "This hunting lodge may have been haunted at one time, but it is no longer. Thank you for finding me and helping me, even though I scared you half to death with my talk." She sighed. "I'm just a crazy old woman."

Andi patted her hand. "Maybe so, ma'am, but no matter what, you did save my life. And I saved yours. Let's call it even and just enjoy Christmas while you're with us."

Maddie's black eyes filled with tears. "You've got yourself a deal, dearie."

Andi nodded and smiled at the lady trapper. In spite of having been lost, hurt, and scared, she had a feeling that this icy Christmas was one of her best ever.

She grinned at a new thought. *At least, it will be after I pay Melinda back for that snowball she slipped down my neck at the railroad station. Hmm, I should probably make a new list of notes on how to do that just right.*

She couldn't wait to get started.

Did You Know?

The Lone Pine earthquake really happened. Also called the Owens Valley earthquake, it struck on March 26, 1872, at two thirty in the morning. Historians believe the earthquake hit with a magnitude somewhere between 7.4 and 7.9. It was one of the largest quakes in California's recorded history (the famous San Francisco earthquake being of similar intensity). Twenty-seven people died in the quake and fifty-six were injured. Lone Pine's population at the time was about 300. The quake leveled nearly every building in town, along with quite a few in the other towns of Inyo County.

6. Andi's New Year's Gala

Chapter One

Fourteen-year-old Andi Carter reread her most recent journal entry and sighed. She'd had her journal almost a year now and decided that her sister Melinda's Christmas gift had actually been a good idea.

> *December 30, 1882. Last year at this time, the whole family stayed on the ranch, on account of Taffy's imminent foaling. She foaled on January 2, 1881, so Shasta is almost a yearling. Sunny is with Macy in Arkansas. Macy is not a very good letter writer, but I did finally get news last fall that Sunny and she had made it safely to Aunt Hester's and everybody seems happy with the reunion. I wish I had another foal due this New Year's.*

Alas, no foals were due anywhere on the entire Circle C. Chad had managed the breeding season to avoid any foaling during the Christmas and New Year's holidays. *Why?*

Andi fumed, slamming the journal shut. "Because Aunt Rebecca had a conniption fit when our family did not join her last year for the New Year's festivities in her mansion on Pacific Heights," she confided to her mare.

She did not stuff the journal in its usual place behind Taffy's feedbox. Instead, she held on to it, planning to take it along on this ill-fated holiday trip.

Mother usually declined holiday invitations because of ranch duties, or she took short ones with only Melinda and Andi, leaving the boys behind to run the ranch.

This year was different. She'd promised Aunt Rebecca the entire family would join her for an extended New Year's visit.

"Andi, let's go!"

Mitch's hollering brought Andi to her feet. She brushed bits of straw and hay from her traveling skirt, adjusted her hat, and hurried from Taffy's stall. "Coming!" she hollered back.

Latching the half-door, she gave her mare one more pat and met Mitch at the barn's double doors. "Where have you been?" he demanded. "We're going to miss the train."

"I wish," Andi mumbled, following her brother out of the barn and into the pre-dawn darkness. The sun had not yet risen, and the winter air chilled her to the bone.

She pulled her traveling wrap closer around her shoulders and allowed Mitch to help her climb up into the family's large surrey. Then he hopped into the front seat. Taking the reins, he slapped the matched bays.

Andi glanced at Mother and Melinda. "You have straw in your hair," Melinda scolded, plucking the unwanted pieces from one of her sister's dark curls.

Andi rolled her eyes and settled back against the seat. It was going to be a long trip to San Francisco. First, the hour-long ride into Fresno, where Mitch and Chad would hire somebody to return the surrey to the ranch.

Next, the eight-hour ride in the railroad cars to Oakland, on the east side of San Francisco Bay. Worst of all, an icy ferry trip across the bay, with the choppy black water slipping over the railings and slapping Andi in the face.

She imagined it all, and it all happened exactly as she knew it would. By the time the ferry bumped into the dock along the Embarcadero and blew its low horn, it was late afternoon. The cloudy sky cast a dark and gloomy look over the city, threatening rain.

"We left in the dark," Andi said wearily, crowding into the carriage Aunt Rebecca had sent to meet them, "and we arrived in the dark."

"Winter days are short and damp in the city," Mother said.

Andi shivered. *Truer words were never spoken.*

The horses clip-clopped up the cobblestone street as if they didn't care about the chilly wind blowing off the bay waters. *They must be used to it*, Andi thought. The carriage soon pulled to a stop in front of Aunt Rebecca's Pacific Heights mansion.

Auntie's home was not as fancy as the Governor's mansion in Sacramento, but Andi's eyes nearly popped out of her head when she saw how the place had been decked out. *I reckon the city folks don't distinguish between Christmas and New Year's. It's all one long holiday to them.*

Aunt Rebecca's coachman, Thomas, along with Chad and Mitch, brought in the family's luggage. Celia, Aunt Rebecca's pert little maid, curtsied then ushered the family to the guest rooms, of which Auntie had several.

"You ladies will be sharing a room this year," Celia said. "Miss Carter has filled the other rooms with many out-of-town guests this year."

Melinda and Andi exchanged wary glances. Then Melinda made the proper response. "That's perfectly all right with us."

Andi quickly agreed. Melinda was a strong anchor in a sea of strangers. Ascending the staircase, Andi counted four people she didn't know.

Where in the world are Levi and the girls? Andi didn't ask this question aloud. With the house bursting with highfalutin' guests, the children had probably been banned to their rooms for the evening.

Andi had just finished unpacking her carpet bag and hung her party dress next to Melinda's in the heavy oak wardrobe when Aunt Rebecca, without knocking, burst into their room.

"Andrea Rose."

"Yes, ma'am?"

Before leaving the ranch, Andi had promised both Mother and herself that she would respect Aunt Rebecca and do as she asked. Sadly, it was getting more difficult the older Andi grew. Auntie's demands increased in proportion to Andi's age. Andi was fourteen now, so who knew what her aunt had in mind?

Thankfully, Aunt Rebeca only wanted Andi's attention. In her next breath, she addressed Melinda. "Melinda Jane."

"Yes, ma'am?" Melinda parroted Andi's response.

"You may finish unpacking later this evening. Hurry now. Celia is announcing supper to Katherine and the children, along with my six guests." She smiled. "I am looking forward to introducing you two." Then she lost her smile and focused her attention on Andi. "Please remember that you are a young lady at the table this evening."

Andi flushed but held her tongue. *Here we go again!*

Chapter Two

Supper flew by, mostly because after her introduction to the three couples, everyone ignored Andi. She sat between Melinda and Betsy, content to sip her soup like a lady and pretend to enjoy the more unusual dishes Celia served, like the escalloped tomatoes and olive oil pickles.

By the time the cream puffs and salted nuts were served as dessert, Andi was too tired to eat them. Mother and Katherine excused Andi, Levi, and the little girls to retire upstairs.

Never was Andi more anxious to leave the company of all those strangers. She walked sedately until she left the dining room, then all four raced up the stairs.

"I'm mighty glad you're here, Andi," Levi panted.

"Me too!" Betsy and Hannah echoed as one.

Levi drew Andi aside before they parted for their rooms. "I just want to warn you ahead of time. Auntie has gone all out for this New Year's Eve celebration. She's got your whole day planned tomorrow, and a busy one it will be."

"What?" Andi's eyes grew wide. "What do I have to do?"

"You'll see." Levi winked and took off down the hall. His giggling sisters followed.

Andi was too tired to give tomorrow's tasks more than a brief yawn. She undressed, curled up under the quilted comforter, and was asleep in an instant.

A brisk knock on the guest room door the next morning roused Andi and Melinda. Thinking it was Celia with a message from Mother or Aunt Rebecca, Andi called, "Come in." She choked back a surprised gasp when their aunt opened the door and entered the room. "Good morning, ladies."

Andi opened her mouth to summon a polite reply when the words caught in her throat. "Auntie, what is *th-that*?" She stuttered, aghast, at the creature held tightly in her aunt's chubby arms.

Melinda, suppressing a giggle, poked an elbow into Andi's side and said nothing.

Aunt Rebecca smiled. "Why, this is Pookie, my dear." She jiggled the little beast in her arms and tickled him under his furry chin. Two dark-brown eyes peered walleyed at Andi.

"He is my new companion," Aunt Rebecca gushed. "I read just recently how her majesty, Queen Victoria, is known for her great love of pets, especially of dogs. She brings them into her home at Westminster and treats them like one of her children." She smiled wider. "I have employed a maid to care for Pookie's needs."

Andi bit down so hard on her lower lip that she was sure it would bleed. A maid for a *dog*? And not a pretty dog, either. Even Prince and King, the rough-and-tumble Circle C ranch dogs held more charm than this furball. For sure he was useless.

It made no difference. Auntie was still Auntie. "Why do you need a dog or another maid?" Andi finally asked, only to receive another be-quiet nudge from Melinda.

"To follow Queen Victoria's example. She too employs a maid for her many furry friends. That's where I got the idea."

She hiked Pookie up close to her face and brushed his ear. "To cap our New Year's Day festivities tomorrow, I have taken the liberty of inviting a photographer to capture my Pookie and me, along with a portrait of our entire family."

Andi was rendered speechless. What would Chad think when he learned he must pose alongside a mutt–er–dog with Aunt Rebecca? She caught Melinda's amused look. *She's thinking the same thing.*

Now, that would be something worth seeing.

Aunt Rebecca gave the girls no more time to ponder this strange turn of events. Instead, she was full of blustery orders this morning. After all, she said, today was New Year's Eve.

"Come along, my dears," she ordered. "We have much to do before the rest of our New Year's Eve guests arrive, as well as the guests on New Year's Day."

Guests? More guests? Were they not all properly installed in the various guest rooms on all four floors of this mansion already? Aunt Rebecca planned more guests for tonight and the next day?

Andi wished more than ever that she was home standing watch over a laboring mare. She pulled back the covers and stood beside the bed. Melinda followed suit.

"What do you want me to do?" Andi asked. She hoped it was nothing more than straightening the wrinkled coverlet on their bed, hanging up her clothes, and maybe dusting.

Aunt Rebecca set Pookie down. He immediately waddled over and licked Andi's bare foot. *Ugh!* She wiped off the dog spit with her other foot and sat down on the bed, pulling her feet up and under her nightgown.

Andi did not care for dog kisses of any kind, but she supposed being licked on the foot was heaps better than being licked on the face.

"We must make sure that all of our traditional New Year's customs are taken care of before this evening. I have jotted down the do's and don'ts on this list."

She pulled a scrap of paper from her pocket and frowned. "Hmm, most of these have already been seen to. Let's see, what did I have in mind for you girls?" She tapped her ample chin and peered at the ceiling, as if the answer hung from the chandelier.

Then she looked at her list and began half reading, half reciting from memory a long list of New Year's customs most of which Andi had never heard of and did not know why they mattered.

She was about to ask "why," but her tongue stuck to the roof of her mouth. *I will write these down in my journal to remind me never to celebrate the New Year with Auntie again.*

Aunt Rebecca looked down at her list to refresh her shaky memory. "Clean the house prior to New Year's." She clucked her tongue. "Oh, yes. The staff is taking care of that."

Thank goodness, Andi breathed quietly.

"Take out all of the trash, every bit. Hmm, yes, Thomas and the others are tending to that task."

She peered at her list and kept reading.

"Clear the hearths so new fires can be lit on the first day of the New Year." She looked up. "I have set your brothers to that task."

Lucky them. They'll end up full of soot.

"They will be sweeping away the soot of all of last year's 'ills' and ushering in a new year with a clean slate."

Aunt Rebecca beamed.

Pookie, with the tap-tap-tapping of his claws on the hardwood floor, was sniffing around for more bare toes to lick. Andi kept her toes well out of reach.

"Make sure you have a new item of clothing to wear, Andrea. And you too, Melinda."

"Why?" Bold, brave Melinda asked.

"Why, to symbolize fresh beginnings. Otherwise, you risk bad luck the rest of the year." She clucked her tongue as if risking bad luck was a terrible fate.

Andi let out a breath. "Mother bought me a pair of riding gloves for Christmas. Does that count?"

Auntie nodded, too distracted to really hear what Andi asked. If she had paid attention, it was doubtful she would have agreed to such a breach of New Year's etiquette.

"You didn't bring along your new riding gloves to the city," Melinda whispered from across the bed.

"Auntie doesn't know that," Andi whispered back.

Thankfully, Aunt Rebecca was still not paying attention. She was too busy infusing her nieces with silly New Year's customs. "We must listen for the church bells to ring out exactly at midnight." She looked seriously at Andi. "To chase away evil, you know."

No, Andi didn't know.

"Oh, yes." She smiled and planted her finger on one of the spiderly lines of text on the paper. "Here we are. This is important, so listen carefully. Right before midnight, Andrea will take charge of the large fruitcake."

"What?" Andi asked, startled. "What fruitcake?"

"At the very stroke of midnight, the front door will be flung open and we all shout "Welcome, welcome" to bring in the new year. Then you, my dear, will throw the fruitcake against the front door to ensure a year without hunger."

Andi gasped, bewildered. Why would anyone throw a sticky, heavy fruitcake against a front door just as the church bells were ringing? "But Auntie, why must I—"

"Oh, one last thing." Aunt Rebecca eyed the girls with worry. "Has your mother or Justin given you money for your pocket?"

Our what? Even Melinda looked befuddled at this strange question.

Auntie did not miss the look on their faces. "You girls must scurry off to ask Justin for the coins. Everyone, even small children, must have money in their pockets, in order to ward off misfortune in the coming year."

"May we dress first?" Andi asked innocently.

Aunt Rebecca didn't hear the question. She scooped up Pookie into her arms, hurried out to the door, then turned for one last word. "Don't forget to ask the cook for that fruitcake!"

After Aunt Rebecca left, Melinda and Andi collapsed onto the bed and let their giggles turn into loud laughter. "Have you any idea what Auntie was going on about, with customs and that superstitious nonsense?" Melinda asked.

"No idea," Andi said between guffaws. Auntie's odd list of New Year's traditions and customs had set her head spinning. "As soon as I'm dressed, I'm going to find Justin and ask what in the world any of these customs have to do with bringing in the New Year."

Sadly, she couldn't find Justin. He'd gone downtown to check in at his San Francisco law office. Everybody else seemed too busy to bother, so Andi sucked in a breath and got to work.

Chapter Three

December 31, 1882

Never did a day last so long nor had been so tedious, not to mention silly. By the time Aunt Rebecca ran her family and her staff ragged with all of her New Year's preparations, Andi was so tired all she wanted to do was go to bed.

However, she was not allowed to slip away. Maybe if Andi were six or seven years old she might get away with finding a soft bed or a sofa and snooze, but rumors flew that here in San Francisco any boy or girl over the age of ten always partied until midnight or even longer.

Back on the ranch, everyone was too tired to do more than say "See you next year" when the family headed for bed at their usual time. It was a Circle C joke. Chad always gave the cowhands the night off and sent them into town with a special monetary gift. "I know you won't be back here until next year!" he hollered as they rode off. They laughed and waved, grateful for such a generous boss.

After things quieted down, Melinda played the piano and the family sang their favorite hymns. Andi especially liked "What a Friend We Have in Jesus." When all the singing was over, the family ended the evening with "Auld Lang Syne."

Best of all, they knelt together and put the old year, with all its hardships, behind them. Mother or Justin prayed that God would bless the new year. Then the family headed to bed. New Year's Day was a workday on the Circle C ranch, except if the day fell on Sunday. Then it was off to Sunday services.

This city's New Year's Eve festival was shaping up to be something completely different from anything Andi had ever experienced in her simple ranch life. She knew Aunt Rebecca was a dedicated Christian woman. Why else would she always harp on her young niece to behave like a Christian young lady?

Andi soon learned that many of Auntie's guests did not act like Christ-followers. But as it was not her own home, nor Mother's or Justin's, she did not say a word. Elderly relatives were respected, even if they acted a little crazy.

Rebecca's overnight guests from Los Angeles were not the problem. No, indeed. It was the strangers from this city, the drop-ins who just wandered inside as New Year's Eve grew closer.

Andi had no idea that on New Year's Eve in the city, the wealthy people up and down Nob Hill and Pacific Heights (and probably other places) always threw their homes wide open. Clearly, the saying, "the more the merrier" was an honored theme.

To Andi, it was like "the more the noisier."

Ladies and gentlemen, while conducting themselves in a manner worthy of visiting Rebecca Carter's home, flooded in and out without an invitation or calling card. The maids and kitchen staff were hard-pressed to keep up with the food and drinks.

Children of all ages ran up and down the stairs and slid down the banister railings. Levi, Betsy, and Hannah didn't look shocked at all.

"Aw, Andi," Levi said, laughing. "I've had two years of this since we moved in with Aunt Rebecca. I'm used to it now. It's not so bad, just part of city life."

He grabbed a hat off the hook and darted out the door.

"I'm off to see my chums the next street over," he said. Then Levi was gone, without a word to Kate, his mother, or to Aunt Rebecca.

As the evening wore on, Andi wore out. Levi returned looking stuffed and tired. Andi made sure she had that dratted, silly, dark fruitcake nearby, so she could have it in hand as midnight approached. She just wanted to throw the dumb thing and retire.

Levi caught Andi's *why am I doing this?* look and laughed. "I threw the fruitcake last year. It made such a mess. Fruitcake flew everywhere—raisins and nuts and goo. Don't worry. You don't have to clean it up. That's what the maids are for. And the birds and squirrels get most of it."

"It's like everybody goes a little crazy on New Year's Eve in the city," Andi retorted.

Grinning, Levi couldn't agree more. He appeared to be enjoying every minute of it.

As midnight approached, Andi's uneasiness rose sky high. Everybody looked at her with expectation, as if they were counting on her, Andi Carter—and Andi Carter alone—to make sure that Aunt Rebecca's household was spared poverty or misfortune. *What a silly tradition!*

She listened for the church bells and watched for the moment when the door would be thrown open.

Midnight came. Sure enough, church bells from all over the city began to chime at once. No one could miss them. It sounded like the entire city was alive with pealing bells. Everyone shouted, "Ring out the old, ring in the new!"

Andi stood on the porch, transfixed at the sound.

In the distance, far out over San Francisco Bay, dozens of fireworks shot into the air. Red, blue, green, and yellow.

What a sight!

Andi was so taken by the sights and sounds that she nearly forgot her cue. The open doorway and the "Welcome, New Year!" shout brought her back to her senses.

I feel so stupid, she thought. Then with all her might, she hurled the large, heavy fruitcake toward the front door.

Splat! The cake hit the door dead center. It crumbled and fell every which way. *What a waste of a good fruitcake!*

A cheer rose, along with applauding. A crowd three or four rows deep of strangers spilled out of Aunt Rebecca's and onto the porch. Others from the sidewalk hurried up her wide steps and shoved their way into the confusion.

Andi was not prepared for what happened next.

Everyone paused and listened for the church bells to go silent. As the last stroke died away into silence, every person young and old, large and small, boys and girls, and men and women, pushed into each other's arms and gave each other kisses.

Andi stared, her mouth agape. Then she shoved her way past legs and billowing dresses. There was no chance anybody would give Andrea Rose Carter a New Year's kiss.

Never! The idea was barbaric, common, and wanton.

Too late. A boy about Andi's age grabbed her by the shoulders as she pushed past him and . . . he kissed her. Then he stepped back and shouted, "Happy New Year!" He was gone in a flash, headed for another young girl on the sidewalk.

Andi was so surprised that she stood like a halfwit. Bad mistake. By the time she escaped inside the house and ducked into the kitchen, two more boys had caught and kissed her.

Unbelievable! She was so angry and humiliated that she buried her head on the kitchen counter and burst into tears.

"Andi?" A quiet voice spoke above her ear. Mitch's voice. "I saw you run indoors. Are you all right? The boys don't mean anything by it."

"Don't they?" she sputtered between sobs. "An easy way to take advantage of a girl without getting into trouble."

Mitch's hand squeezed her shoulder.

"I reckon I'm a spoilsport with all these odd customs," Andi whispered, sniffing back her tears. "But stealing kisses just because it's New Year's doesn't seem right. It smacks of Johnny Wilson's bad manners a year ago."

Mitch pulled her up and into a brotherly embrace. "At least you didn't punch any of *these* youths." He chuckled.

Andi sniffed back her annoyance. "I don't even know their names. It's . . . it's—" She couldn't think of a word bad enough to describe what she had just been put through!

"The city folks are used to this kind of thing," Mitch said softly. "I don't care for this silly folderal, and I doubt Mother is happy. I'm sure she will decline Aunt Rebecca's offer of any future New Year's Eve festivities. Stick close to me, Sis. I won't let it happen again."

He released her and held out a hand. "Come along. We're singing 'Auld Lang Syne,' and then everybody is retiring."

At last! I can go to bed! Andi clasped Mitch's hand and looked up into his face. "Thanks, Mitch."

By the time Andi dried her tears and lost the flush in her cheeks, she was ready for the final "bringing in the New Year." The street crowd had disappeared, and only Aunt Rebecca's overnight guests remained.

Everyone gathered around the table for a final hot drink, then around the piano while one of Auntie's guests played "Auld Lang Syne."

> Should auld acquaintance be forgot
> And never brought to mind?
> Should auld acquaintance be forgot
> And days of auld lang syne?
> For auld lang syne, my dear
> For auld lang syne
> We'll take a cup o' kindness yet
> For days of auld lang syne.

Everybody sang all of the verses. Andi knew only the first and last. For the last verse, everybody linked arms and sang with deep feeling. This brought tears to her eyes and she was ready to forgive Aunt Rebecca for the ruckus she allowed to overtake her mansion that night.

When the last notes fell away, an older gentleman offered a prayer for the new year, just like back home on the ranch.

That's when Andi forgave Auntie all the way.

As she climbed the stairs, made ready for bed, and cuddled under the bedcovers next to her sister, Andi thought, *Thank goodness that's over.*

She could not have been more wrong.

Chapter Four

January 1, 1883

After a busy day getting everything in order for New Year's Eve, then the noisy and rambunctious night, plus the bewildering tradition of fruitcake throwing and rude boys stealing kisses, Andi slept well into the next morning.

When she rose, she rummaged around in her valise and pulled out her journal. Then she climbed back into bed and sat up against the headboard. It was the first time since arriving that she had a moment to catch up and record a few things about New Year's Eve she that did not want to forget.

Andi had not liked much about last night except for the singing of "Auld Lang Syne" and the fireworks over the bay. She was hoping for a relaxing day, with the only bump in the road being Aunt Rebecca's plan to gather the family for the photograph taken with Pookie.

She was dotting the "i" in Pookie when Celia knocked on the bedroom door. "Miss Andi, Miss Melinda!"

Beside Andi, Melinda jerked awake. "Where's the fire?" she mumbled, yawning.

Andi giggled. "No fire. Just Celia. Come in!" She closed her journal and set it on the bedside table.

"The Missus Carters are wondering why you two ladies have not risen and are still abed."

Melinda and Andi exchanged wary glances. *What now?* Melinda struggled to sit up and asked, "Why shouldn't we be? It was a very late New Year's Eve."

At nineteen, Melinda had her I'm-in-charge voice down perfectly.

Celia took a step back. "Oh, forgive me, Miss Melinda, but the open house begins at noon. That is only two and a half hours from now. You were expected at breakfast hours ago."

"What open house?" Melinda and Andi asked at the same time.

Celia reached into her apron pocket and pulled out a newspaper clipping. "I am so sorry. This is all my fault. I was so busy this morning that I forgot to awaken you earlier. You two must hurry. The other ladies will be arriving soon."

"What other ladies?" the girls asked in unison.

Melinda reached out and snatched the clipping out of Celia's hand. Her cheeks reddened when her eyes scanned the newspaper announcement. "Heavens above!" she breathed softly, using one of Aunt Rebecca's expressions. "Listen to this, Andi."

Then she read the clipping.

NEW YEAR'S CALLS. MISSES MELINDA AND ANDREA CARTER, ELIZABETH SWANSON, AND LORINDA AND ANNABELLE FIELDS WILL RECEIVE WITH MRS. JAMES CARTER AND MISS REBECCA CARTER AT THE HOME OF THE LATTER, NO. 135 FILLMORE STREET, FROM NOON UNTIL 6 P.M. TODAY, JANUARY 1.

Melinda let the clipping slip from her fingers and onto the coverlet. "Why didn't Mother or Aunt Rebecca warn us?"

Just then, Betsy ran into the bedroom. Her cheeks were flushed with excitement. "Get up, sleepyheads. You can't receive gentlemen callers in your nightgowns."

Melinda threw back the covers and leaped from bed, clearly determined to meet the challenge of being ready. Andi, however, picked up the clipping and gawked at it. She was only fourteen. Betsy was not yet nine years old.

"Whose idea was this to receive gentlemen callers?"

Instead of leaping onto the bed, Betsy sat down on the edge like a young lady. It was easy to see why. She was slicked up as pretty as a picture in a white dress with a blue sash. Her straight brown hair had been curled with irons, and a huge blue bow pulled back the stray strands. The maid had been thorough and Betsy looked adorable.

But definitely *not* old enough to receive callers.

Betsy saw Andi's look and blurted, "Auntie took out an ad in the *San Francisco Examiner*. She didn't tell Grandmother or Mama or any of us until early this morning, after Uncle Justin read it in the morning paper at breakfast. Then the beans got spilt."

"That's for sure," Andi mumbled.

Betsy giggled. "You should have seen Grandmother's face. 'What have you done, Rebecca?' she asked, nearly dropping her teacup. Uncle Justin just chuckled and shook his head, like it was quite amusing. I think it's grand!"

"Wh—" Andi could not get her words out. She swallowed and tried again. "What's it all about?" she finally managed. She looked for Celia to explain, but the maid had slipped out of the room.

It was up to Betsy to explain what was going on.

"It's the most exciting thing . . . nearly as exciting as New Year's Eve," Betsy gushed. "Young ladies of marriageable age, and families too, which is what Auntie has planned for us, since of course except for Melinda, you and I and my friends are *not* marriageable age yet, can announce that we will be at home during certain hours to receive calls on New Year's Day."

She slid from the bed and grabbed Andi's arm. "Hurry, Andi. Get ready. Buggies full of young men, and any boys past the age of ten, will soon be arriving. I hope that handsome boy from next door, Brody, will visit."

Brody? Andi remembered Brody from when she was a little older than Betsy. Brody was younger than Andi, but they'd had good times chasing his cat, Cleo, and climbing the apple tree in Auntie's backyard years ago.

Betsy was clearly not interested in climbing trees today. Or chasing a cat. She kept up her non-stop chatter. "Plus, my friends Lori and Anna will be gathering here with us, so it will be almost like another party!" She spun around, causing her white chiffon skirt to splay out in a wide swath.

"Hold on, Betsy." Andi caught her arm. "Tell me about this custom so I don't look like a fool." *Like I felt last night.* But she didn't add that part.

"Young men from all over the city read the newspaper ads," Betsy said in a rush. "They sometimes come calling one at a time, but most come in bunches. You can see their buggies from far off. They're dressed like they're going to a ball. They like to come and eat refreshments, drink gallons of lemonade and coffee, and talk to the ladies of the house."

She giggled. "Even me this year!"

Betsy leaned closer, and her voice dropped to a whisper. "The young men love calling on the rich, fancy folks up on Pacific Heights and Nob Hill. Aunt Rebecca has had the staff cooking to show off such a table that they will all go away happy and remembering us."

Andi bit her lip. *Thank the good Lord I live in the valley, far away from these crazy city social customs.*

The fact that Mother had not warned her daughters about this custom convinced Andi that Aunt Rebecca was up to her old tricks—plunging Andi into the correct social expectations whether she wanted to or not.

Andi sighed and shoved the covers away. "I suppose there is nothing to be done about it but accept it gracefully." She grinned. "I wouldn't mind seeing Brody again. Did he come around last night? I don't remember seeing a red-haired boy in all that crush."

Betsy shook her head. "Uh-uh. He was out making the rounds with Levi and the other fellows." Then she brightened. "He'll come today. He's thirteen, old enough to go calling on young ladies. All each gentleman needs to bring with him is a good supply of visiting cards. He leaves his card with each of the ladies he visits. I bet you and Melinda will get the most cards, especially Melinda. Why, she's almost an old maid—"

Andi clapped a hand over Betsy's mouth. "Hush. Melinda will be back from the washroom any minute. You're behaving like a silly goose over these boys. What's gotten into you?"

"Living in the city, I expect," Betsy replied. "And going to that fancy young ladies' school Aunt Rebecca pays for. Miss Whitaker's Academy. The girls are all silly gooses there, except for Anna and Lori."

Her eyes turned round. "Oh, my! I've got to run. Mama set me to a few tasks before my friends arrive. I meant to pop in and ask you if you liked my new dress."

"It's very pretty," Andi assured her. Then she dragged herself out of bed and followed Melinda's example.

167

January 1, 1883, much later
I have survived my first (and hopefully last) New Year's Day calls. I never thought I would admit this, but the day was actually quite amusing. The best part? The young men (and boys) never stayed more than fifteen minutes. Why not? They had dozens and dozens of visits to make, and San Francisco is not small.

All afternoon, Aunt Rebecca's parlor and foyer spilled over with gentlemen guests of all ages. Old Dr. Wilcox and his dear wife dropped by too. When they appeared, Andi realized this was more visitation of friends and neighbors rather than an exclusive time for an introduction to courting time.

She glanced around the parlor. Big sister Katherine was receiving her share of calling cards from eligible bachelors, even from a number of widowers.

No matter what Kate says or does, I know her heart is still with that scoundrel, Troy. For politeness' sake, she might not advertise that she's not available, but Andi knew not one of those calling cards would be kept.

Mother collected a few too. When Andi thought about Mother entertaining even the idea of marrying again, her stomach twisted in dismay. "How awful," she whispered to Justin in the horror of the moment.

"Let her enjoy the attention, honey," he chided her. "It's Mother's business with whom she visits, not yours or mine, or which gentleman's visiting card she chooses to keep."

Andi kept quiet after that, but she couldn't help giving some of those older "dandies" a sidelong glance. Would any of them be invited to the Circle C later in the new year?

Her cheeks grew hot just thinking about it.

Most of the young men flocked to Melinda, and why not? Andi did not begrudge her pretty sister even one calling card. She was marriageable age, and now that Jeffrey Sullivan the Rat was gone, why shouldn't she enjoy the polite attention? And the handsome gentlemen were so very polite! Melinda, to her credit, always knew what to say to make anyone feel at ease, even the shy, clumsy-looking fellows.

Betsy and her school chums received callers too. Their greatest joy focused on which girl collected the most calling cards. None won that contest, so all three would remain best friends. All three girls held the same number of cards, six each, from the six boys over the age of ten and under the age of fourteen who came calling on them that afternoon.

Andi had collected her share of visiting cards as well, at least a dozen and maybe more. A couple of the young men pressed a polite hand against hers when they left and gave her a hopeful smile. She stuffed the cards in a spare pocket to take back to school. Everyone would laugh their heads off when they learned how the city folks celebrated New Year's.

She drew out one of the visiting cards and spent a few minutes examining it. WALTER D. ADAMS.

Andi knew nothing about this boy and could not even remember what he looked like. They all looked alike in their black jackets and top hats.

"You are conducting yourself in a manner that makes Aunt Rebecca giddy with joy," Chad whispered in Andi's ear when he and Mitch returned from their own visiting rounds.

Justin, the lucky duck, did not have to go with them. He was immune. He had married last September, and he and Lucy spent their time helping Aunt Rebecca and Mother entertain the many guests.

Andi suspected that big brother was also keeping a keen eye on Melinda, Betsy, and Andi, along with Betsy's young friends. With Justin present, the gentlemen, young and old, remained gentlemen.

The gentlemen callers partook liberally of Aunt Rebecca's hospitality. A huge table was spread in full view between the parlor and the foyer. They couldn't miss it even if they tried. It was handsomely decorated and displayed all kinds of dishes to suit a gentleman's taste, but only a few specially chosen cakes and confections.

In a spare moment, Andi approached the table and asked, "Why so few desserts?"

Aunt Rebecca huffed, "Those are entirely out of taste for an occasion like this."

Surprised at her aunt's shocked tone, Andi looked over the spread. She did not recognize most of the dishes and was afraid to taste anything. Then Mother stepped in and told Andi their names, pointing to each one in turn.

- scalloped oysters
- cold tongue
- turkey
- chicken
- ham and pressed meats
- boned turkey
- jellied chicken
- salads and cold slaw garnished with fried oysters

- bottled pickles
- French and Spanish pickles
- jellies
- charlotte-russe
- ice cream
- two large white cakes just for decorating the table
- baskets of sponge cake
- fruits, nuts
- hot chocolate with whipped cream
- coffee
- lemonade

Mother heartily approved of no alcoholic beverages being served. "The young men could become tipsy after visiting so many homes if everyone served such beverages," she said when one of the older gentlemen inquired.

"Oh, I see." He bowed politely and took his leave.

The callers seemed to have enjoyed the hospitality. The first batch of gentlemen finished their round of refreshments and light conversation. They checked their timepieces and bid the ladies good-bye right on time, around twelve-fifteen. In and out, as promised.

After bidding them good-bye, Andi kept the door open. Three fellows were heading up the walk. The departing men adjusted their top hats, brushed down their woolen coats, and made no attempt to lower their voices. "Hullo there, Robert," one fellow greeted the next group of visitors. "They are good cooks in this house, as you will shortly discover."

Robert stepped through the wrought-iron gate and waved. "By thunder, I'm ready for some warm apple pie and a good cup of coffee."

Sorry, Robert, Andi thought with a grin. *No apple pie here.*

One companion slapped Robert on the back and tipped his hat at Andi as they strolled past. "I'll just take coffee," he responded. "You may have had no champagne last night, but I did. This is much too early to be paying calls on ladies."

"Buck up, Stephen," Robert responded. "We're just getting started. The list in the *Examiner* is long this year." He pulled a clipping from his coat pocket, glanced at it, and shoved it back inside. "Ah! New Year's Day!"

Andi smiled, followed them inside, and shut the door.

January 1, 1883, late evening

The family photography session with Pookie did not take place, for which I'm sure my brothers are happy. It seems Pookie was allowed to wander around during the visiting hours from noon to 6 p.m. Pookie is friendly, and he imbibed too many morsels of rich food from the callers. As a result, he became ill. Aunt Rebecca put her "poor dear" to bed and said he must have rest and quiet.

Andi closed her journal, packed it away in her valise, and settled herself under the covers for a restful night's sleep.

The whole family left early the next morning to catch the ferry to Oakland, where they would board the railroad cars to Fresno at nine o'clock sharp. This meant Aunt Rebecca would not have the time to recall the photographer and take the family photographs, even though this morning Pookie had recovered from his New Year's celebration.

Not even Mother sounded sincere when she bade Aunt Rebecca good-bye and apologized for not being able to take the time to stay for the photograph. "We cannot miss the ferry," she explained.

Tears glistened in Aunt Rebecca's eyes at this missed opportunity. She held Pookie and promised "the dear lad" that the family would gather soon for a photograph.

Not if I live to be one hundred, Andi hoped. She gave Levi a quick hug and whispered, "Maybe Aunt Rebecca can hire the photographer, after all. He could take a portrait of you, the girls, and Pookie. That would be mighty special. Shall I suggest it to her?"

Andi rubbed her stinging arm all the way to the carriage. Levi's pinch would stay with her until she boarded the ferry. Laughing, she climbed into her seat and waved good-bye.

Note: Everything mentioned in this story is taken from real-life, Victorian New Year's Day customs and celebrations of the 1800s.

Turn the page to learn more about Andi's adventures on the Circle C ranch in the Old West.

The Circle C Series

Circle C Beginnings - Meet spunky, six-year-old Andi Carter, who is eager to grow up and experience the Wild West in 1874. Exploring the Circle C ranch with her friend Riley, meeting Indians, and a visit to the state fair are a few of Andi's adventures. Ages 6-9

Circle C Stepping Stones - Andi is nine years old, and her filly Taffy is three, the perfect age for them to finally become a horse-and-rider pair. Join Andi's adventures on the Circle C ranch with her family and friends in 1877 California. Ages 7-10

Circle C Adventures - Living on the Circle C ranch in 1880 is a dream come true for twelve-year-old Andrea "Andi" Carter. Follow her latest escapades as she stumbles in and out of trouble and learns life lessons from her strong and loving ranching family. Ages 9-13

Circle C Milestones - Andrea Carter is back in this series for older readers. More exciting adventures with an older, teen Andi, on the Circle C ranch in 1880s California. Will she finally realize her dream of helping run the ranch, or does God have other plans for this spunky young woman? Ages 11 and up.

Read sample chapters and download free learning guides for all the Circle C series at:
CIRCLECADVENTURES.COM

Join Andi fans for stories, contests, and fun on Andi's blog!
ANDICARTERSBLOG.COM

Made in the USA
Middletown, DE
25 October 2022

13418447R00099